Ransom

Banker Amos Fillmore's life is shattered by the brazen kidnapping of his pretty daughter, Anita. The kidnappers, led by the notorious gunman Earl Weathers, demand a ransom payment that can only be raised if Fillmore raids the assets of his Crater, Arizona bank. In the end, though, even that payment is not enough.

Duplicity and violence rage while Anita remains hostage in a cave carved deep into the hills of the desert wilderness. Her safety is secondary to avarice, and even those tasked with upholding justice are inept and overcome with greed.

It seems as though neither Anita nor her ransom will ever be recovered from the grip of the desert. That is until the territory's top gun, Laredo, steps in. . . .

Ransom

Owen G. Irons

A Black Horse Western

ROBERT HALE · LONDON

Robert Hale Limited
Clerkenwell House
Clerkenwell Green
London EC1R 0HT

www.halebooks.com

Typeset by
Derek Doyle & Associates, Shaw Heath
Printed and bound in Great Britain by
CPI Antony Rowe, Chippenham and Eastbourne

ONE

Crater was not much different from half a hundred similar towns scattered around Central Arizona. It had its share of corruption, crime and violence, of despair and baseless hopes for a thriving future. Located on Thorne Creek, a tributary of the Gila River, the town of Crater suffered through the dry spells and by mid-summer Thorne Creek was reduced to a trickle – wells were in demand. Fortunately for the citizens of Crater the water table was relatively close to the surface and fairly reliable.

There was a crater after which the town was named. A sinkhole some two hundred yards across, it was some distance from the town centre, located near the flank of the jumbled broken hills where only grey brush and an occasional wind-tortured pinyon pine tree grew. Newcomers went out to look at the sinkhole, stared at it for a few minutes and never returned to look again: as landmarks went, it wasn't all that interesting.

Crater itself had four stables, a blacksmith's shop, two general stores, a saddlery, two hotels (high and low class), an elected town marshal, a bank, a stage station where the disheartened could catch the coach out of town, a yellow brick courthouse still under construction, and eleven saloons.

Crater had its malcontents and plain human refuse, but it also boasted a number of responsible, civic-minded citizens dedicated to seeing Crater grow and expand healthily.

Just now one of these citizens, the respected town banker, Amos Fillmore, was in his place of business stuffing loose cash into a muslin flour sack. Fillmore had married early and his first wife had given him a charming baby child named Anita. The marriage had been felicitous, and when Louise had passed away of consumption when the child was only three years old, Fillmore had been devastated. Not wanting Anita to grow up without a mother's counsel, nor wishing to remain alone himself for the remainder of his lifetime, Fillmore had married again. This marriage, to Florence, had not proven so felicitous. The charming young lady he had met at a church picnic had proven herself to be a grasping, shrewish nag before the wedding cake had been cut.

There was nothing he could do about that but suffer; he could do something for Anita, however. Now a young woman approaching twenty years of age, she had few promising suitors in the derelict town of Crater. But there was a far more serious problem to consider just now, and it would take money to resolve it – a great deal of money.

Tad Becket had forgotten his hat on leaving the bank, and once outside had spun almost immediately to retrieve it. The young teller had been working there for only six months, but Mr Fillmore had told him often that he showed promise. Twenty-five, narrow, his light hair already thinning, Becket wore spectacles that he did not absolutely need and was diffident in the extreme, especially when dealing with female customers. He was proud of his appearance and conscious of his position, which led him to retrace his steps to the bank. It was not seemly for a banker to walk around town bareheaded.

The door to the inner office was slightly ajar, and Becket set out towards it. The movements within halted him in his tracks, though. He saw . . . thought he saw . . . could not have seen Mr Fillmore shoving stacks of currency into an old flour sack. Tad was sure that there was a reasonable explanation for Fillmore's action. There must be, but it was to say the least, highly unusual. Tad should simply poke his head in and enquire, but he could not bring himself to do so. He slipped back outside into the glare of the brilliant sunshine.

The day was hot even for July as Tad Becket walked slowly along the plankwalk toward the Sierra Restaurant. He carried his nagging doubt with him. What had he seen? Amos Fillmore absconding with bank funds! Ridiculous. But what if it were so and Tad failed to report it? If he made an accusation that proved false, he would certainly lose his job. If what he suspected was true and he did not report Fillmore, he might be subject to some sort of criminal charge himself. He needed to talk to someone about it, and quickly, before Fillmore could make his escape, if that was what he had in mind.

Fortunately he saw Bill Thatcher entering the Sierra as he approached the diner. He could talk to Bill. The young deputy marshal was about Tad Becket's own age. Bill had tried to teach Tad how to fish, how to shoot, although Tad had no natural talent for either. He would ask Bill what he should do.

'Why shouldn't he be bagging up some money?' Bill Thatcher asked as they sat facing each other across a square table in the Sierra.

'I don't know. I've just never seen him do it,' Tad answered nervously, moving his elbows as the waitress served them both coffee.

'Could be a big cattle sale in the works,' Bill Thatcher suggested, 'or some mine operator taking out a large loan he doesn't want publicized. A lot of people wouldn't want it known that they had that kind of cash on hand.'

'I grant you that,' Tad said in a quiet voice, his eyes darting from place to place before settling again on the rugged-looking young deputy. 'But nothing like this has ever happened before.'

'Does Fillmore tell you everything about the bank's affairs?'

'No, of course not, Bill . . . but. . . .'

'But it bothers you. All right, Tad. I won't tell Marshal Pepper about this yet.'

'No, please don't!' Tad was somehow terrified of the bulky town marshal with his glittering black eyes and meaty torso. Bill smiled gently.

'I'll just hang around the back of the bank awhile and see what's up, though I think you've just gotten a touch of imagination.'

'I suppose you're right,' Tad Becket said as the waitress returned to take their orders. 'I hope you're right.'

They ate in silence for a while – ham, potatoes and corn on the cob was the lunch special. When he had nearly finished, Tad changed the subject by asking, 'How are things going with Anita?' For the young deputy was crazy in love with Anita Fillmore, as everyone except Anita seemed to have noticed.

'I don't know,' Bill shrugged. 'I've been watching and waiting for her to come into town, shopping or something. Screwing up the courage to talk to her a little more plainly, but I haven't seen her for a couple of days.'

'It's the heat. Ladies don't like to come out in weather like this.'

'I suppose you're right.'

'Have you considered riding out to her house some evening?' Tad asked. Bill shook his head.

'I feel about Amos Fillmore something like you feel about Marshal Pepper. I'd as soon not encounter the man. Especially if he had an inkling of my intentions.'

'Why, Bill? Is there something he doesn't like about you?'

'Besides the fact that I'm a young man stuck in a dangerous, low paying job.'

'Oh.'

'Yes, "oh". Fillmore is waiting for some respectable, secure man with a good deal of money tucked away in his bank to come asking for his daughter's hand. And if anyone knows how much money I don't have, it's Amos Fillmore.'

As he fished two silver dollars from his pocket to pay for their meals, Tad Becket said, 'About my situation – you haven't forgotten, have you, Bill?'

'No. I'll keep an eye on the bank for the rest of the day unless something more urgent comes up. You just relax, go back over there and count your nickels.'

Amos Fillmore suffered through a long, hot afternoon. He found the heat more oppressive than usual. His lips were parched; his head throbbed. He went about his duties woodenly. Twice he filed loan documents he had forgotten to sign, once he found himself at a loss trying to recall the name of an elderly woman he had known for twelve years as she made her small monthly deposit. Fillmore watched the round

11

clock on his office wall as it ever-so-slowly ticked off the lethargic minutes.

He was in it deep now. He only wanted to flee the bank, to have done with it all. He wondered if the glances Tad Becket cast his way didn't carry the look of censure, of suspicion. Those concerns he dismissed as the shadows of a criminal's guilty mind. He could not dismiss his own censure, but what else could he do!

At five o'clock with the summer sun still riding high and bright in the sky, Amos Fillmore recovered his derby hat from the rack, straightened his tie and smoothed back his hair. He strode to the outer office where young Tad Becket stood waiting by the front door. Fillmore thought the young, slight clerk's eyes still held an overly-curious gleam, but that was only nerves – had to be.

'Good evening then, Becket,' Fillmore said as he turned to lock the door to the bank behind them.

'Good evening, sir,' Tad Becket responded woodenly. He saw that Fillmore carried no sack, that there was no tell-tale bulge under his coat. So, then, perhaps Bill Thatcher had been right. Tad was imagining things. What reason, after all, could Amos Fillmore have for embezzling bank money?

He was a well-respected man with a fine home, family and friends. The sort they called a pillar of the community. It made no sense that he would risk all for a sackful of money. Possibly Tad had done the man an injustice. Perhaps he had even observed Fillmore in a moment of weakness which his common sense overrode upon reflection. It made no difference. Tad had seen no crime committed; he had no further obligations in the matter.

Bill Thatcher yawned and glanced at his steel pocket watch again. He had been resting in the shade of the cottonwood grove that flourished near the back of the bank, along the course of Thorne Creek which was now only a sandy wash with scattered, scum-filled ponds here and there. Five o'clock and there had been no activity near the bank. By now Amos Fillmore would have left the bank, and after recovering his horses and surrey from the Crater Stable, would be driving home.

The young deputy marshal rose, stretched the kinks out of his muscles and started toward his piebald horse tethered nearby. He had decided to follow Fillmore, just in case something not apparent was up. Marshal Herb Pepper had not sent anyone looking for him. Thatcher knew that it would take a raid by an army of outlaws for Pepper to move more than from his office to the One Tree Saloon and back on a day like this when heat hung oppressively over the sun-beaten town.

Glancing toward the western road out of Crater, Bill saw the banker's rig moving away from the town, his high-stepping matched bays drawing the vehicle towards the enclave where Crater's better citizens had built their houses among a vast grove of scattered oak trees. Bill swung into his saddle, knowing that there was little chance of his detective work having any positive result. That did not matter.

It gave him an excuse to ride towards the Fillmore house. Who knew, he might surprise Anita Fillmore who often went riding at this hour. The image of Anita, her fair hair loose, her smile wide and bright as she trotted her prize black across the open land came into Bill's thoughts and he urged his piebald on away from Crater.

If he had held his position for another ten minutes, denied himself the pleasurable vision of Anita Fillmore, Bill might have been able to end matters right then and there, for no sooner was he out of sight than two horsemen appeared from the eastern end of town. One of them held the horses while the other slipped up to the back door of the bank.

As promised, that door was unlocked. The man reached inside, snatched up the flour sack resting there, closed the door again so that its latch caught and returned to his horse, grinning as he held the moneybag aloft.

'No word?' Amos Fillmore asked Florence, his wife as soon as he had entered his house and closed the door with the oval-shaped leaded glass insert. Florence who had been sitting in one of the dark-violet, overstuffed chairs, embroidery-work on her lap, answered without looking up. 'Hasn't been time enough.'

'No, I know it,' Fillmore said, removing his hat, wiping back his thinning grey hair. 'I'm not thinking clearly, that's all. Since they took her. . . .'

'You can't do anything but wait!' Florence snapped. 'Have yourself a glass of whiskey.'

Amos Fillmore's second wife was nothing like Louise, Anita's mother. Louise would be frantic now, rushing to him to seek mutual comfort in the loss of their beautiful kidnapped daughter. At the sideboard where he did pour a tall whiskey for himself, Fillmore reflected that perhaps it was better that the aloof, unemotional Florence was at his side during this crisis. He could always count on her solidly logical response to problems.

Fillmore sagged into a chair matching his wife's. Loosening his collar and tie he took a deep drink of the whiskey and muttered, 'It's been two entire days now. I can't sleep, can't eat. It's in my mind constantly, not knowing what might be happening to Anita.'

'You can't do anything about that,' Florence said, raising her steely gaze to meet the lost look in his watery blue eyes. 'All we can do is wait. You've done all you can.'

Yes, Amos Fillmore thought, taking another deep drink of whiskey. He had done all he could: embezzle money from the bank where he had worked for twelve long years, building the community's trust. Now he was a common thief, a criminal. If caught there would be no forgiveness no matter the circumstances that had forced him into this rash act. . . .

'You haven't let anyone know, have you, Florence? Not even a hint.'

'No one's been around,' she answered, returning to her embroidery. 'And why would I want to say anything and destroy my reputation and social standing?'

Florence spoke these words as if he were a fool

16

for asking. He was a fool, Fillmore decided, for doing what the demand note had instructed. The note which had been pinned to the saddle of Anita's black horse when it returned home riderless. What other choice was there? He loved his daughter, and if it cost him twenty years in prison to save her, well it was a fair price.

If those men let her go. If they had not already. . . .

Amos Fillmore drank again and sat immobile, inconsolable, brooding in the settling shadows of his drawing-room.

Bill Thatcher drew his piebald pony up in the heated shade of a wide-spreading oak tree. He removed his hat and cuffed the perspiration from his forehead. He could just see the Fillmore house, the adjacent corral and barn. No one had stirred from the house. In the corral Bill could see Anita's tall black horse. So she was not out riding on this afternoon. Perhaps it was still too warm. She would prefer the cool of evening. He decided to wait a while longer, hope prodding the decision. Hope that she would emerge from the house and stride prettily to the corral to saddle her horse. Then Bill thought, he would quite accidentally encounter her on the trail. It was time that he spoke some of the things that were on his mind, nagging him day and night.

The shadows began to spread out from the oaks, the sun heeled over toward the western range. The day became noticeably cooler, and a few nightbirds had begun to appear, but Anita still did not come out of the house. The black horse began to roam the corral restlessly as if expecting an exercise run. The house remained closed and dark. Bill glanced again at his watch. He could not waste much more time here. Marshal Pepper would be waiting for Bill to relieve him at the jail so that he could stamp over to the Sierra Restaurant and have his dinner before going home to his room in the hotel.

Weary with disappointment, Bill Thatcher swung into his saddle once more. He sat on the piebald for a few long minutes, watching the house, but no one emerged into the dusk-lighted cool of evening. It was only then that Bill did start to wonder whether something was not amiss. Perhaps Tad Becket had been right. Or maybe it was only because Bill was so disappointed at not seeing Anita Fillmore, but he began to think worriedly that something might be wrong with the Fillmores.

Very wrong.

Wearing a deep frown, he started the piebald back towards Crater as the sky flared up briefly with deep crimson and burnt orange before the sun sank heavily beyond the far horizon.

TWO

Marshal Herb Pepper stood scowling on the plankwalk in front of the adobe building which housed his office and the jail. There was only a last faintly flickering glow of gold along the western horizon. Night was settling over Crater. Pepper spat a stream of tobacco juice pressed from the oversized wad of chaw he had in his cheek. Flat-faced, bulky in body, Pepper was not an amiable man at any time. On this evening he was nurturing less than fond feelings concerning his deputy, Bill Thatcher. The kid knew that he had his supper every night at this time before retiring to his hotel room in the Crater House Hotel. The point had been impressed on Thatcher when he was hired for the job and reinforced repetitively. If there was not a riot in the town, Bill Thatcher was supposed to arrive to take over the night shift. Pepper thought briefly about firing the kid, but there was no one else even vaguely qualified for the job who would accept the low-paying position of deputy marshal.

Pepper let his thoughts wander to happier matters, and for a moment he forgot his anger with Thatcher. Within a matter of months, perhaps weeks, he would be ready to retire comfortably and then he would shake the dust of this ramshackle town from his heels, turn his back on the jail and its problems and the petty annoyances of office.

Pepper was still lost in these more amiable thoughts when Bill Thatcher appeared, riding his piebald horse. Bill's face was apologetic, but Pepper only waved a hand at him, dismissing the explanation. Pepper would not have to endure this much longer – any of it.

'I do need to talk to you for a minute, Marshal,' Bill said after looping the reins to the piebald around the hitch rail. Ducking under the reins he approached Pepper who had already started away. Now Pepper halted and turned back, asking heavily:

'What now?'

'It's just . . .' Bill wasn't sure where to begin. 'Has anyone seen anything suspicious going on at the bank lately?'

'Suspicious?' Pepper frowned heavily. 'What do you mean? Like lurking thieves eyeballing the place? Something like that?'

'Maybe,' Bill said. He had removed his hat. Now he combed his dark hair with his fingers. 'I'm not sure what the trouble is.'

'But you're sure there is trouble?' Pepper demanded. His stomach had begun to growl.

'No, not exactly,' Bill said, and Pepper sighed audibly before spitting out another stream of tobacco juice.

'What then, exactly? Has someone reported trouble, Bill?'

Bill was hesitant to repeat what Tad Becket suspected. It could all be groundless, he knew. He put it indirectly.

'Tad Becket is worried that something is up.'

'Tad Becket is a worrying man,' Marshal Pepper said. 'If you can label him as such. More a boy who wishes he were a man. He's frightened of his own shadow. What's bothering him now?'

Bill remained evasive. 'It was nothing in particular,' he said. 'I was just wondering if anyone had reported trouble at the bank.'

'I don't get what you're trying to tell me, Bill, or not to tell me. When you figure out what it is, come to the Sierra and find me. My stomach and I have an appointment with one of Minnie's steaks.'

Bill made no reply. He had been foolish even to broach the subject if he wasn't going to tell the entire story. But what then? Suppose Herb Pepper had gone to Amos Fillmore and told him that his clerk suspected him of embezzlement. Without proof, there was only the vague concern of a young teller, and Tad Becket might find himself without a job if Fillmore was offended by the insinuation. And why wouldn't Anita's father be offended? One of Crater's founders and one of its most substantial citizens. He would not be pleased to know such a rumour was circulating among his depositors.

Bill loosened the cinches on the piebald's saddle and tramped into the marshal's office, his thoughts already distant from Tad Becket and his theory. All of the three cells were empty, their iron-barred doors swung open. Bill sat in the marshal's swivel chair and tilted back, closing his eyes as he wondered and worried about Anita Fillmore. When he could stand it no longer, he rose and went out, locking the door behind him. He stood for a long minute looking up and down the street which was fairly quiet, there being only a ruckus of some sort in front of the Tooth & Claw Saloon, but then it would have been unusual if there weren't something going on there once the sun had gone down: the boys could have their fun.

Bill Thatcher started uptown toward the group of small cabins which lay in an irregular row beyond the Crater Hotel. If anyone knew if something was wrong with Anita, it would be Dusty Donegall.

Dusty was a few years older than both Anita and Bill Thatcher. With wild, fiery red hair, she lived alone in one of the faceless cabins of this section of town. What Dusty did with her time, how she supported herself was unknown. It was told around town that she was the only heir of a railroad magnate and that she had come West with the idea of buying a small shop – or a section of land, depending on which tale you listened to. But Dusty had done neither of these.

Garrulous and outgoing as she was, Dusty was seldom seen far away from her well-tended cabin unless she was downtown shopping with Anita whom she had befriended, or riding with her across the long country.

Dusty had not been accepted by the uptown families, Anita Fillmore's included, because of her uncertain status, living as she did among Crater's 'lower types.' Bill had heard people asking why, 'If she does have all that money, don't we ever see her spending it?' Bill could have answered that, his own finances being so low as to be tenuous. It was simple: if she spent her money, she wouldn't have it any more. Bill knew nothing of Dusty beyond rumour, except that she could talk a person to death and that she was a good friend to Anita who needed someone to share her woman-thoughts with.

When Bill approached Dusty's cabin, he found the door standing open to the cooling evening air, saw a lantern burning softly and heard Dusty singing an Irish air. He rapped on the door frame. The redhead emerged from the back room where her kitchen was situated, drying her hands on a small towel. Her eyes sparkled as she recognized Bill and she greeted him in her habitual, effusive way.

'Hello there, lawman! Finally caught on to me, did you? Come to arrest me. Sit down anywhere. Knock that lazy dog out of your way. I was just about to take a cherry pie out of the oven. You'll have some, with coffee? How come we don't see you much these days? Where did you get that hat, Bill?'

After he had waited for a while, hoping she would run down eventually – faint hope – Bill interrupted Dusty.

'What's happened to Anita? She's not sick, is she?'

'You know,' Dusty said, pausing to take a breath and poke her fingers into her wild mass of red hair, her eyes briefly becoming worried, 'I've been wondering where the girl is. We haven't been riding for two days now, I wondered if she might be sick, too, because we love our little evening rides, and you know it's good for her to get away from the house, the way Florence just sits there, frowning, the old mummy. . . .'

There was no choice but to interrupt again. 'You haven't been out to the house, then?'

'It's seldom I go out there, Bill. You know the way things are with me and Florence. The woman thinks I have the plague or something, I guess. As for the respectable Amos Fillmore. . . .'

There was no stopping the woman. Bill wondered if Dusty lived alone too much, or if her incessant chatter was the reason she lived alone. Out of the mass of chatter, Bill sifted out the facts that Anita had not been around and that Dusty had not been out to the Fillmore house to enquire. The rest of the barrage of words was just random shrapnel. He managed to make what he hoped was a polite escape. He liked Dusty; it was difficult not to, but she had to be taken in small doses.

He still had not put the piebald away for the night, and that was his expressed excuse for leaving, though it was doubtful if Dusty even heard him say that as she followed him out onto the porch, commenting on the hot weather and the idiots in the capital, a rash she had developed on her back and why couldn't Stottlemeyer's shoe store find anything that was both stylish and a good fit for her small feet? There were a few other comments which Bill mercifully didn't even hear as he touched the brim of his hat and started down the street toward the marshal's office.

Once out of range of Dusty's verbal barrage, Bill's thoughts became gloomy again. Something was wrong at the Fillmore house, he had decided, although he could not guess what it was. Was there a link between Tad Becket's idea that Amos Fillmore was taking money from the back and the fact that Anita had not been out of her house for two days? If there was, Bill couldn't figure it out.

His thoughts were again distracted by the ruckus in front of the Tooth & Claw Saloon which had now spilled from the doorway and the plankwalk into the street. A dozen or so men with beer mugs in their hands were egging on three or four others who were wrestling, cursing and kicking each other. Bill approached them.

'Let's cut this out, men!' he said in a loud voice. Only two or three heads even turned to look at him. 'Let's have some order here. Do I have to call Marshal Pepper?'

'Shouldn't be too hard to find him,' a big man with a toothless grin shouted, nodding towards the saloon. 'I believe he's at one of the back tables.'

Which is where Herb Pepper probably was. Muttering a few words about keeping a lid on things, Bill started out away from the crowd. He was developing a dull headache, probably from the heat, and he was in no mood to try dragging one or two of those roughhouse types to the jail.

The piebald horse eyed him accusingly as Bill again reached the jail. It had been a long day and the animal was overdue for food, water and a rub. Bill unwrapped the reins and walked the mount towards Long Trail Stable, the nearest, dingiest and cheapest of the four in Crater. He found the stablehand outside, looking idly up at the scattered stars.

'Kinda late tonight, ain't you?' the man asked Bill.

'I am, Wink. It was a busy day.'

Wink Rollins nodded and took the reins to the piebald without saying another word. Wink was dependable after a fashion. Things were done promptly if not well. He was a narrow man with virtually no hair and seemingly no vices. He did have one lasting concern, though. The proud owner of a prominent gold tooth, he suffered under the delusion that he would one day have it stolen out of his mouth. From time to time Wink would come to the sheriff's office to report a stranger who seemed to be studying the tooth with too much interest.

Leaving the horse in Wink's hands, Bill Thatcher sighed, hitched up his gunbelt and started off on foot to look in on the other ten saloons scattered around town, hoping that nothing serious was going on at any of the watering holes. The night remained warm as it would until just before dawn and the sky remained clear and star-shot. Bill continued his rounds, his heart heavy and shrunken in his chest, but he was determined now.

Something had happened to Anita Fillmore, and he was going to find her, even if it required desperate measures.

Anita Fillmore sat with her arms looped around her knees, staring into the near darkness of the cave. She leaned against the damp wall of the old excavation and stared at her captor, Ike Morris. Ike was getting restless. He rubbed at his splotched face with a filthy hand. Ike was a true drunk and a few hours away from the bottle sent him into small fits. It would soon be his turn to be relieved, Anita knew.

There were three men holding her captive: Morris, Kyle Trotter, who worked for her father off and on as a handyman, and Earl Weathers with his darkly vicious, pocked face. Weathers, it was said, was a former gunfighter grown too old and slow for the occupation.

It puzzled Anita that none of the three had made an effort to disguise himself in any way. All were known to her and she could name them to the marshal. The only answer seemed to be that they did not intend to give her that chance. This thought chilled her, but she had accepted it, and as time went by she stopped believing that they meant to do away with her. Perhaps they would simply leave her tied in this old mine shaft, forever undiscovered.

After a while Kyle Trotter arrived to relieve Ike Morris who was off like a shot towards the nearest saloon. Ike sat on the old wooden chair beside the wooden table where a low-burning lantern flickred.

'Want a drink of water, Anita?' the fat man

asked. He seemed kindly but if so, what was he doing with these kidnappers? She knew that Trotter was lonely, for he talked the night away, ruing his wasted life. Maybe Trotter thought that money could relieve his loneliness. Perhaps it could.

Anita shifted her position and Kyle Trotter's eyes flickered her way. She was not trying to slip the rope from the strong knots that held it on her wrists. She had given that up after the first day. She knew that she could only watch and wait for rescue.

Where was the marshal?

Where was Bill? Did he even know that she was missing? Was he thinking about her at all? She wondered if he ever thought about her as she thought of him these days. Anita's father had refused to consider Bill as a suitor – Florence had decided Bill was not a suitable match. It seemed these days as if her father acquiesced to Florence on every point. Perhaps he feared losing her, although Anita would not mind if her stepmother disappeared tomorrow.

She wanted Bill! People would not label him handsome, she supposed, though his face was well-formed, his dark eyes direct and open. He was lean, perhaps over-lean and at times he was clumsy but that was only due to youth and distraction. The only objection to Bill Thatcher was that he had little money. But he worked every day and tried his best at a difficult job. It was hardly his fault that the town was too miserly to pay their lawmen a decent wage. Her stepmother had said that Bill was no more than a night watchman, rattling shop doorknobs to make sure they hadn't been left open. How would she know? Neither Anita nor Florence ever went into Crater at night when the wilder element was running in the streets.

'I once had a wife,' Kyle Trotter said out of the near-darkness and Anita sighed inwardly. She had heard this portion of the fat man's life three times in two days. He droned on; she was not listening at all.

Anita had decided that Kyle Trotter had been chosen for the gang because of his familiarity with the Fillmore house and their habits. He would have known what time Anita went out of a morning to see to the horses. It was after her father had gone to work one day, before Florence had risen from her bed, that they had taken her. The three had worn bandannas on that morning only, perhaps fearing outside discovery.

Once back at the cave – one of dozens of test shafts the ore companies had dug over the years –

they had made no attempt at all to conceal their identities, calling each other freely by name. They also spoke boldly of their plans for spending the ransom: far-off places were mentioned, likewise women they had once met and a small parcel of land that was for sale at a bargain price. They seemed to have no doubt at all that they would succeed. And Anita herself . . . would the one who found her skeleton in the years to come even know her name?

Where was Marshal Pepper?
Where was Bill?

THREE

Jake Royle had bad feet. He liked his boots off whenever possible. He had them removed now as he sat behind his desk, believing the man facing him was unaware of it. Actually there wasn't any mistaking the source of the odd smell in the small office which served as the enforcement branch of the Territorial Bank Examiner.

Laredo was used to his boss's ways. They had been working together for a long while. Once, a long time ago, Laredo had found himself down and out. He had been eyeballing a small bank in a small town called Cannel. Laredo was hungry, tired and broke. While he stood considering the bank as a solution to his troubles, a man who moved on cat feet slipped up beside him in the hot shade of the alleyway and introduced himself.

'Jake Royle's my name,' he said, stuffing the bowl of a stubby pipe with tobacco.

'Pleased to meet you,' Laredo replied shortly. He was not in the mood for a stranger's idle conversation.

'Working in town, are you? Royle persisted, lighting his pipe.

'Not at the moment.'

Royle nodded, blew out a stream of tobacco smoke and studied the tall stranger. 'I, myself, am employed here,' he said. Laredo cast an annoyed glance at the stocky man. 'For the present, that is. I travel all around,' Royle continued, indicating all of the territory with a wave of his pipe.

'What are you, some kind of drummer?'

'No. I am employed, my young friend, as an operative in the enforcement arm of the Territorial Bank Examiner's office.'

'Oh.' Laredo felt cornered suddenly. The inoffensive little man stood watching him quietly. Laredo wondered how Royle could have known what he had in mind that hot, dry desperate day.

'Yes,' Royle went on, 'you know men will try to stick up these little banks in isolated areas. Then they make their break toward Mexico, California, anywhere, free as birds. The local law doesn't have the time nor the resources to expend hunting them down. Me,' Royle said with a gnome-like smile, 'I've got all the time in the world. All the time in the world.' With that the little man nodded and walked away. Laredo stood watching his back. If that had not been a warning, it was the next thing to one.

It wasn't until late afternoon that Laredo traced Royle to his hotel room where he sat shirtless, bare feet propped up.

'Mr Royle,' Laredo had said, 'how's chances of getting hired on at a job like yours?'

Since then Laredo and Royle had travelled many miles together. Now, Jake Royle had surrendered to age and his bad feet, and held down the office while Laredo and a handful of other enforcement officers handled the field work.

'What do you have for me?' Laredo wanted to know.

'I want you to get down to Crater,' he said. 'It's a little town not far south of Flagstaff. The accountants are already on their way, sent off this morning.'

'What's happened?' Laredo inquired, wrinkling his nose. He was no longer surprised at Jake Royle's method of finding comfort for his sore feet, but he would never grow accustomed to it.

'We're not sure anything has happened as yet,'

Royle said, leaning back to stretch his arms. The tall, sharp-featured man seated across the scarred desk watched Royle with curious eyes. 'It's like this, Laredo, a deputy marshal in Crater has sent us an interesting telegram. There is some suspicion that the bank manager there has been pilfering money, and a simultaneous suspicion that his daughter might be missing.'

'Suspicions?' Laredo said, 'are we now reacting to suspicions?'

'If this deputy marshal' – Royle turned a sheet of paper on his desk and read the name – 'Deputy Thatcher is correct in his surmise, we may be able to save a young woman's life if we act quickly.'

'You say the deputy marshal reported this. Why isn't his boss looking into it?'

'I would guess that the deputy doesn't have any faith in his superior's abilities, wouldn't you? Besides, a local lawman can't go off half-cocked because some prominent citizen is accused of something. You know how few really able men fill those roles, Laredo. Most town marshals are some kind of relative of the mayor or someone else of stature, or broken-down old saddle tramps who are weary enough of travelling to accept a low-paying job which requires little in the way of gumption or intelligence. Often a town marshal is appointed precisely because he has the ability to turn a blind eye when it comes to local bigwigs.'

'If we went out investigating every suspicion. . . .'

'Good,' Royle said, 'I knew you'd agree with me. Besides, Laredo, you've been living the good life too long. Lying around here, collecting your wages for doing nothing.'

'There was the small matter of that bullet in my hip,' Laredo commented drily.

'Yes, but that's all healed now, isn't it? It's not a long ride to Crater, Laredo. Go down there and take a look around. If this Fillmore has tapped the bank's reserves, our accountants will find out soon enough. If there is anything to the suspicion that his daughter has been kidnapped, well, that's your area.'

'I feel sorry for Fillmore,' Laredo said. 'If his daughter was kidnapped, they offered him no choice but to collect the ransom money. Does that mean he'll be judged leniently?'

'I'm not a judge, Laredo, and neither are you. At the very least the man will be disgraced, but there's nothing we can do about that. What we can do, will do, is recover the money and bring that girl back alive.' He hesitated – both men knew the ways of kidnappers – 'If that's possible.'

Laredo walked out into the brilliant sunshine. His leg was still stiff from the bullet he had taken in his hip, but he supposed that Royle was right. He had hardly been earning his keep laying up in town. The enforcement branch of the Territorial Bank Examiner's office paid him for doing precisely the sort of job Royle had laid out for him. Normally it would be just to recover the money, if there were indeed any missing, not to recover a kidnapped victim, but Royle could not draw such a distinction, nor could Laredo if it came to that. In fact, finding the girl seemed the more urgent facet of the investigation.

Walking heavily toward the stable where his big chestnut horse was kept, Laredo again wondered what was wrong in Crater. The town marshal might not be worth much, but surely he should have been notified if the deputy was suspicious enough to wire the bank examiner's office. Perhaps he was simply intimidated, fearful of losing his job. It took all kinds, Laredo decided with a shrug.

His chestnut had its head hung over the stall, eyeing him accusingly. Its look seemed to say, 'Finally! How long was I supposed to stand here waiting for you?' Laredo stroked the big horse's neck by way of apology, smoothed the blanket over its back and leveraged the saddle up. That small effort caused some discomfort in his still-aching hip. He supposed that was something he would just have to get used to, like lingering arthritis.

By noon Laredo was on his way south across the long land, heading the horse towards Crater and its troubles.

'What is it, Bill?' Tad Becket asked excitedly. The two men sat at their regular lunch table in the Sierra Restaurant. 'Did you find anything out?'

'No,' Bill Thatcher said in a low, morose voice. He turned his coffee cup between his palms and looked up at the young bank teller. 'I did something a little crazy, and I thought you ought to be warned.' He paused, swallowed hard and told Tad: 'I sent a wire to the Territorial Bank Examiner's office.'

'God, Bill!' Tad Becket said, his eyes appearing stunned. 'Did you mention my name?'

'No,' Bill said, unsurprised but disappointed by Tad's temerity. Did he fear losing his job that much? 'I suppose Herb Pepper will fire me. At least he'll give me a chewing like you've never seen, but what was I to do, Tad? It's not just the fact that Fillmore might have been taking money from the bank, but what I believe it might be for – Tad, I think Anita Fillmore is missing.'

'Missing?'

'I think she's been abducted. No one's seen her, not me, not even Dusty Donegall.'

'She might have just gone out of town,' Tad suggested. The fright had returned to his pale eyes.

'She didn't take her horse. She sure didn't board a stagecoach. If she were going out of town, she would have told Dusty. You know how close those two are.'

'You think the two events are tied in together.'

'I think they *might* be,' Bill said. 'That's all I told the Bank Examiner's people. I just don't know, Tad. I know you're worried about the bank, but I am out of my mind with the fear that something's happened to Anita.'

Tad was shocked at the idea that someone had kidnapped Anita, but it was the bank that bothered him more immediately. We all worry first about disasters that are closest to home. Anita was not family, the bank was his home. A vague sense of guilt shadowed Tad's thoughts as he considered this seemingly callous view, but he let it pass.

'When?' he asked weakly. 'When are the examiners coming?'

'This afternoon probably,' Bill told the haggard looking teller. 'Whatever you do, don't warn Amos

Fillmore that they're arriving.'

'No,' Tad said, smoothing his thin pale hair. 'No, of course not.'

'I just thought you should know.' Bill Thatcher said. Rising from his chair, he added, 'Tad, if you've ever borrowed a nickel or two from the bank, now would be the time to account for them.'

'I would never!' Tad said with wounded dignity. 'How could you even suggest such a thing, Bill. Of me, your friend?'

'I'm not suggesting anything,' Bill said, fitting his hat onto his head, 'just telling you – because you *are* my friend.'

Tad Becket was anything but mollified as he went out onto the street in front of the Sierra. The traffic along the street was normal for mid-day when he started back towards the bank. Approaching his workplace he saw two smallish men wearing derby hats, both wore brown town suits, both carrying briefcases. They were nearing the front door from the opposite end of the street: the bank examiners. Bill groaned inwardly.

Amos Fillmore glanced up from behind his desk and smiled warmly at the two well-dressed men who had entered the bank. 'What can I do for you gentlemen today?' he asked.

They told him.

Tad Becket suffered through the long day in the hot interior of the bank. He overheard Amos Fillmore alternately stuttering with indignation and lowering his voice to a low reasonable appeal. The bank examiners answered each outburst with the same toneless voices. The two men, Tad learned from glancing through the search warrant they had presented, were named Cassidy and Stolz. They looked so much alike in their brown suits, performed their task in the same methodical manner that it was difficult to tell them apart. Each had a narrow mustache sketched across his pudgy face. Amos Fillmore stood over them for an hour or so as the two went through the bank's records, page by page, line by line. Then he returned to the outer office where he stood, fists on his hips staring with dark speculation at Tad. The hands on the clock ticked slowly past. The examiners stayed on until after closing time, requesting no refreshments, not pausing to step outside of the office for a breath of air.

'You might as well get out of here,' Amos Fillmore said grumpily to Tad. 'If they have any questions for you, they'll come calling.'

'Is there . . . have they found anything amiss, Mr Fillmore?'

'I don't know,' Fillmore answered in a tone of

voice that indicated that he had already surrendered to the certainty that they would find what they were looking for. Ned gratefully took his hat from the hook where it had been hanging and made his escape from the bank. Fillmore stood watching his teller as the young man ambled away. Beyond him, across the street, stood Marshal Herb Pepper.

Amos Fillmore inclined his head and the marshal nodded his understanding.

'Oh, Mr Fillmore,' a voice within the bank called, 'a word with you please.' Fillmore took in a deep breath and turned to face his accusers.

It was something like closing the barn door after the horse is gone, Herb Pepper thought as he slowly walked the length of Main Street following Tad Becket. But Tad couldn't be allowed to get away with it. Besides, there might come a time when they summoned Becket to testify to what he knew. Amos Fillmore was a clever man. It could be that he had come up with a way to explain the missing money. Then Becket would be the only witness to the crime.

They knew that it must have been Tad Becket who alerted the bank examiners simply because he was the only other man working at the bank. Besides, Herb Pepper remembered the somewhat confused questions Bill Thatcher had been asking about trouble at the bank. Becket and Thatcher were friends. Who else could have asked Bill to enquire into the bank's affairs?

It was a damn shame it had come to this, the marshal thought. Only one more day and it would have all been done with and no one the wiser. But now the cat was out of the bag. And Tad Becket was responsible for it. A slowly building anger toward the teller simmered in Herb Pepper's brain. All of the planning, all of the work only to have Becket wreck it with one telegram.

Pepper wondered what the teller had told Bill Thatcher. Bill, too, would have to be watched closely. Once the marshal began worrying over what had, just hours before, seemed a foolproof plan, concerns began to multiply.

What if Earl Weathers and his two flunkies decided that their share of the money was not large enough and decided to simply ride away with the whole take? What if something went wrong with their treatment of Anita Fillmore. For example, a rope left tied too tightly for too long? What if they just rode off and didn't tell Fillmore or anyone else where they had left the girl?

For the moment those possibilities were out of the marshal's control. He did not even know where they had taken the girl. And now was not the time to go looking for her. One thing at a time, he told himself. If there was to be any sort of formal hearing – which seemed inevitable – Tad Becket would not be attending it.

He would be unable to.

Pepper could not take care of this job himself, but there were plenty of drifting toughs at the One Tree Saloon or the Tooth & Claw – any of the other drinking spots. Men who needed drinking money and weren't particular how they earned it. Pepper had used such hoodlums a time or two in the past when he had a personal grievance to settle. It was safe enough – the hired men did not dare cross the marshal. To do so would only result in them being thrown in jail, Herb Pepper's word against that of a common street thug.

Every man has his uses. Herb Pepper strode slowly toward the Tooth & Claw Saloon.

Bill Thatcher rode on across the broken land. He had lost the horsemen's sign a long while back, but continued in a direct line, guessing that the riders he was following would be apt to set a straight course and follow it.

In the early morning, before the Fillmores had risen, Bill had ridden to their house. Knowing that

Anita was probably taken from the paddock as she tended her horse or prepared for a ride, he had started his search in the soft earth there. It had not rained in weeks, nor had there been any traffic in the area to erase the obvious signs of three horses that had been tethered in the oaks beyond the corral. Three men at the house, their horses concealed in the grove. They had to be those he sought, and though the tracks were now three days old, Bill could make them out so long as the earth was yielding enough to accept them. Now, riding the rocky land south of the folded, brush-clotted hills, just west of the crater, he found the going difficult. The soil was sun-baked adobe clay and basalt gravel.

Whether the men had chosen this route purposely or by sheer chance, the rocky terrain effectively hid signs of their passing. Where would they have been going? Bill held his piebald up, letting it breath. He squinted into the low sun, wiped his brow and tried to put himself in the kidnappers' position.

With little success.

They could have doubled back towards a hideout near Crater or made a bee-line for Flagstaff or any of the other dozen or so scattered outposts in the area where they might have friends os associates. Knowing *who* they were might have helped, but Bill could not guess their identities, although it would seem they must be familiar with Crater, familiar enough to know that Anita's father ran the bank and to know where the Fillmores lived. Maybe that was not the case. Maybe they were passing outlaws who used a few carefully-worded enquiries to gather all that information in seemingly innocuous conversation with the local people.

The odds, Bill decided, were more in favour of their being locals. Were any of Crater's well-known badmen acting strangely, had any suddenly quit showing up at their favourite saloons? Discovering that would take a lot of detective work, and there was no time for painstaking investigation. Anita had been missing for three days now. She was out there alone, suffering and frightened.

The kidnappers, by all reckoning, must have already received the ransom they had demanded. Logic dictated that they would even now be riding hard away from Crater. Had they left Anita on her own to suffer and possibly perish, or taken her with them for reasons of their own? Muttering a bitter curse heard only by his piebald horse, Bill Thatcher continued his lonely search of the bleak land, hoping for some chance clue to Anita's whereabouts.

Anita rubbed her wrists. Deep crimson grooves had been cut into them by the rope that tied her. Kyle Trotter allowed her ten minutes unbound to restore her circulation. The others were unconcerned with her discomfort. Earl Weathers, the pocked wolfish gunman who was obviously the leader of the gang was utterly indifferent to her needs. She was only an object to be returned to its owner when the time came, whenever that time might be. The drunk, Ike Morris was also unconcerned with her pain – the fire in her wrists, the painful stiffness in her shoulders, but in Ike's case it was because he was either passed-out from alcohol or awake and fidgeting, worrying about when he would be relieved so that he could take his next drink.

Kyle Trotter, lonely, fat and kindly, always removed the binding ropes for a few minutes when it was his turn to stand guard. Anita was nice to the man, but wary. It was difficult to say what the source of Trotter's solicitude was. Was he a decent man trapped by events, a gentle person by nature, or did he perhaps have other expectations of Anita? The woman was young but not ignorant. She kept Kyle Trotter at arms' length, careful not to smile too warmly at the fat man.

Something was about to break, Anita was sure. She had heard Earl Weathers telling the others that there was no sense in waiting around now. They 'had it'. By that she deduced that a ransom had been paid for her release, although no one had ever told her that that was what had been expected. A clever girl, she also had figured out that the only one who would pay a ransom for her was her father. And there was only one place he could come up with a large sum of money. The bank.

Even if Anita were to survive, her father would be ruined. She thought fondly, sorrowfully of Amos Fillmore; the man had not had much luck in his life. She recalled her mother dying young, his marrying the terrible Florence and now the kidnapping. And next for him – prison more than likely. Anita did not dwell on what her own fate was likely to be.

Sundown cast curlicues of cloud like crimson dragons' tails across the western skies. Tad Becket glanced westwards, unable to enjoy the remarkable beauty of the flaring colours with which the dying sun painted the filmy clouds. He wandered the streets of Crater aimlessly, dismally. The bank examiners had done their job and left on the afternoon stagecoach. They had not interviewed him. But Amos Fillmore had closed the bank early and walked away slump-shouldered, his face carrying a defeated look. Tad had to wonder whether he still had a job. If the bank failed, it would mean uprooting himself again and travelling down an uncharted road to nowhere looking for another position just when he had gotten himself settled comfortably in Crater. And what kind of references could he present to a prospective new employer? Tad found himself wishing idly that he was a drinking man. They were able to push their worries aside for at least a night, or so he was given to understand. He decided that it would be a good idea to have another talk with Bill Thatcher. Perhaps the deputy had new information on the situation. At the least, he would find a friendly smile, an understanding listener.

Tad stepped from the boardwalk in front of the Crater House Hotel and entered the alley separating the hotel from the Long Trail Stable. It was there that he was jumped.

The rush of boots across the sandy soil was swift and threatening. Tad spun, raising his arm across his face too late to halt the first blow of the fist which landed squarely on the bridge of his nose. His vision blurred and hot blood flooded his mouth and chin. Stumbling back Tad was slammed up against the wall of the hotel and heavy fists were driven into his ribs on either side, their thudding drove the wind from his lungs. Tad tried to scoot along the wall, to escape the beating, but he was no match for his attackers who rained blows on his head, neck and shoulders as Tad cowered, covering his head with his arms in futile defence.

The sound of the gun being touched off was so near at hand that the echo of the shot seemed to roll through Tad's head. When the hands released him he sagged to his knees and then fell over onto his side to lie still in the shadows of the dusk-lit alleyway.

FOUR

'They're gone,' a strange voice said. Opening one eye tentatively, Tad saw the shadowy figure of a tall man who was just now holstering his staghorn-handled Colt revolver. 'They took to their heels at the shot. Do you need a hand up?' the stranger asked, bending lower to examine Tad.

'I think . . .' Tad panted. 'Yes, if you don't mind.' A strong hand wrapped itself around his and Tad was assisted to his feet. He leaned against the wall of the stable, breathing raggedly. His nose was clotted with blood, his ribs ached with each breath.

'What was that about?' Tad asked in a faint voice. 'Who are you?'

'They call me Laredo,' the stranger answered. 'As to what that was about, I haven't an idea if you don't. I just rode into town. I was looking for the marshal's office. Someone told me it was over this way.'

'It is,' Tad said. He still held one arm across his belly. 'That's where I'm going if you want to walk along with me.'

They found a trail-dusty, dispirited Bill Thatcher sitting behind the marshal's desk when they reached the office. Herb Pepper had gone, keeping to his strict schedule.

'What in the world!' Bill asked, springing to his feet as Tad Becket, assisted by a lanky, dark-eyed stranger entered the office. *What now?* was what Bill was thinking. Was there any mercy in this world?

'A couple of toughs beat him up,' Laredo said as he helped Tad Becket into a chair. 'I just happened to be passing.'

'Who was it, Tad?' Bill asked with concern.

'I don't know,' Tad said, dabbing at his nose with a bloody handkerchief. 'I don't think I'd even recognize them if I saw them again. It all happened so quickly.'

'But why . . . and who are you?' Thatcher asked the tall man.

'Call me Laredo. I'm down from the bank examiner's office – enforcement branch. You, I take it, are Bill Thatcher.'

'That's right,' Bill said, taking Laredo's hand doubtfully. 'But you're not one of the. . . .'

Laredo laughed. 'No, I'm not one of those bead-counter types. My job is to try to sort out what you might call the physical side of the problems.'

'Arresting Fillmore?' Tad Becket asked with some apprehension.

'No, sir. To try to recover the bank's money. And to try to find the missing girl.'

'The missing girl,' Tad said blankly. He glanced at Bill Thatcher who nodded.

'Anita. I told you before that I was concerned about her. Now I'm certain that she's been kidnapped, Tad. I think that's why Amos Fillmore took the bank's money. There's no other earthly reason why he'd risk it.'

'I see,' Tad answered dully.

'Now, then, Thatcher,' Laredo said, seating himself on one corner of the desk, 'suppose you tell me what has happened, and what you fear has happened. And what I can do to help you solve matters.'

'I don't know what you can do,' Bill said with a sigh. He sagged again into Marshal Pepper's chair. His own body ached. He had suffered through a long day searching on the open desert for Anita Fillmore. 'I'm glad you're here, though. This has all gotten to be too much for me.'

'And on top of that you still have your duties here in town.'

'Yes, I'm really restricted in what I can accomplish,' Bill said disgustedly.

'Well I'm not,' Laredo told him. 'This is my full-time job for now. Point me in the right direction and let's see what happens.'

After leaving the battered Tad Becket resting in his room, Laredo and Bill Thatcher continued uptown at the deputy's suggestion.

Bill told Laredo, 'You see, there is still no firm proof that Anita has been kidnapped. No ransom note has been found that I'm aware of, no complaint has been made by Amos Fillmore – I assume his silence was one of the stipulations of the ransom demand. That's why we're going where we are.

'Anita's best friend is a woman named Dusty Donegall. She may have seen Anita or heard something from her by now.'

'But you doubt it.'

'I doubt it.' Bill trudged along in silence for a while. Finally he asked, 'Does anyone else know that you're in town, Laredo?'

'Only you and the teller, Becket. In your communication you seemed a little cautious about even mentioning this matter to Marshal Pepper.'

'Herb Pepper is ineffective, lazy and susceptible to influence.'

'Is he criminal?'

'I don't know. I have no proof that he is, but he can be motivated by money. He showed no interest at all in what Tad witnessed at the bank, but that might have been because of the way I was forced to put it to him. I had nothing to go on but Tad Becket's word and Tad himself was tentative in his suspicion. I didn't want to come right out and tell Pepper that Tad was the one making an accusation.'

'I see. Then I'll just leave the marshal out of it as long as that's possible,' Laredo said. 'No one else in town knows I am here. I haven't seen anyone except a strange man at the stable who took my horse and then spoke to me through such tight lips that I could barely understand him.'

Bill laughed. 'That would be Wink Rollins. He's afraid that someone is going to steal his gold tooth.'

'That would explain it,' Laredo replied with a smile. 'Have you any idea at all who might have taken Miss Fillmore or where they could be holding her?' Laredo asked.

'None,' Bill said with passion. 'I was out

searching today. I found where the abductors had left their tracks near the Fillmore house, but I lost them out on the desert.'

'How about Mrs Fillmore? Have you talked to her? She must be frantic if her daughter is missing.'

'Stepdaughter, and no I haven't talked to Florence Fillmore. I doubt she's exactly frantic with concern. More likely she'd have a private celebration if she knew Anita was missing.'

'No love lost?'

'None. Florence Fillmore is a greedy, grasping woman and Anita, not she, stands to inherit whatever Amos Fillmore has – which won't be much after this mess, will it? Here's Dusty Donegall's cabin. Pay no attention to her if she talks your ear off before we ever get to ask her a question. She's a nice lady, but she can talk!'

The door to the cabin stood open. They could hear Dusty singing. A small white dog greeted them, quivering from head to tail. Bill called out to Dusty who appeared from the kitchen with a small stack of dishes in her hands. She opened her mouth to greet Bill . . . shut it again and stood silently watching with wide blue eyes as Laredo followed the young marshal into the house.

'Hello, Dusty,' Bill said, removing his hat. 'This

is a friend of mine, Laredo.'

'Bill,' Dusty murmured. She backed away from the two men, her eyes still fixed on Laredo. Bill frowned, and without hesitation got to the reason for their visit.

'Dusty, have you found out anything about Anita – anything at all? Have you heard from her? If you've given her your word to keep a secret or something, please break your promise. We're seriously concerned about her.'

'Nothing,' Dusty said in a voice as dry as desert sand.

'Have you been out to the Fillmore house?' Bill wanted to know. Dusty hesitated before answering:

'No.'

'Well,' the young deputy said to Laredo, 'there's nothing we can do but search somewhere else, is there?'

'Sorry,' was what Dusty said as the two men started toward the door. Her lower lip seemed to tremble as she escorted them out onto the small front porch. Walking along the dusty road toward the marshal's office, Laredo broke his silence.

'Was that woman all right, Bill? You told me she was a real chatterbox. She seemed scared of something as if she had been threatened.'

'She wasn't frightened,' Bill said, placing his

hand on Laredo's shoulder. 'Dusty was just kind of shocked into silence. Didn't you notice, Laredo, her eyes never met mine. She couldn't take them off of you!'

Laredo smiled with one corner of his mouth and shook his head. 'Let's stick to business, Bill, shall we?'

'Yes. What did you have in mind? You know I've got to stay around town and watch out for trouble.'

'I know. I'm going to try tugging at a few loose ends and see if I can't unravel something. The first thing, I suppose, is to talk to Marshal Herb Pepper. He's acting in a peculiar way for a town marshal with one of his leading citizens in serious trouble.'

'What would you expect him to do?' Bill asked as the two stepped up onto the plankwalk in front of the Crater House Hotel. 'Lock Fillmore up on suspicion alone, which is all there is at this point?'

'No, but I'd expect him to say something to you, maybe to discuss it with Fillmore, at least to have been notified about Anita.' Laredo shook his head, 'It all smells funny to me.'

'To me as well,' Bill said as they continued their way toward the jailhouse past the laughing, cursing crowd across the street at the two saloons, the Tooth and Claw and the One Tree. 'But bucking Herb Pepper is tricky work, Laredo. He's the king of his little empire. He holds all the cards.'

'I'm the joker in the deck then,' Laredo said. 'I don't work for Herb Pepper. You might have to tread lightly, Bill, but I don't mind stepping on a few toes. I'm here to recover the bank's money and to find Anita Fillmore. I intend to do both, Pepper be damned.'

At that moment Herb Pepper was not in Crater. Immediately after leaving his office he had straddled his bay mare and ridden northward, intending to beat Amos Fillmore to his house. He needed to talk to Florence before Amos got there. It really didn't matter if the banker interrupted them after he had had his meeting with her; Pepper could always tell Amos that he was there waiting to talk to him.

Reaching the vast oak grove, Herb guided his horse toward the Fillmore house. Amos's buggy was not in evidence. The marshal rode directly to the front of the house, swung down and made his way heavily to the front door. He knocked twice and the door was opened by Florence Fillmore, her dark face set, worried. She stepped into his arms and hugged him tightly.

'You shouldn't be here,' Florence Fillmore said, looking up into Pepper's eyes. 'You promised that until this was over. . . . '

'It should be over by now, Florence!' Herb Pepper said, holding the woman at arms' length as he studied her almond shaped eyes. 'What's happened? That's what I've come to find out. Those men have had plenty of time to split the ransom money and deliver our share.'

'I don't know what they're doing,' Florence said, shaking her head worriedly. 'I've been watching out the window for the better part of the day. Earl Weathers told me—'

'Weathers,' the marshal said with disgust, 'I knew it was a mistake bringing him into this.'

'Who else was there, Herb?' Florence Fillmore asked. Her fingers were now toying with the buttons on the marshal's shirt. 'He's tough enough, bold enough—'

'And treacherous enough,' Herb Pepper interrupted angrily. He smiled apologetically, 'I'm sorry, Florence. It's not your fault, I know. You did your best, but you and I should be away from Crater by now. Or at least have the money tucked away so that we are ready to go when the time's right.'

'We can't leave before Amos' trouble is settled one way or the other,' Florence said. 'It would look too suspicious if we just pulled up and left right now.'

'Yes, I know it,' Pepper said, tipping back his hat. He drew Florence near and hugged her tightly again. 'I don't know how we ever got tangled up with a man like Earl Weathers. He's a hard man with a rough background.'

'Yes, well we needed that sort of man, didn't we, Herb? I told you how it came about. He came by looking for work one day and we started talking – about nothing really – and the idea somehow came up. I've been so unhappy here, and I know you have too. Sneaking around as we have, neither of us with enough money to make a break for freedom.'

Herb Pepper thought that matters had evolved in a slightly different way. Probably Earl Weathers had come up with the idea on his own and drifted it in front of Florence to see what she thought. Well, what Florence thought was simple enough: her husband was nothing special, but he did have some money, yet all of that was to go to the brat, Anita, in the event of his death. Besides that there was only the bank money. Florence had spent hours thinking about the thousands of dollars that passed between her husband's fingers every day. Enough to free her from the monotony of life in Crater. Enough so that Herb Pepper could resign from the dangerous drudgery of his job. Of Anita,

Florence gave little thought. If something were to happen to the girl, she would only be that much wealthier.

'Earl's got to figure a way to get the money to us – and to deliver the girl,' the marshal said. 'If anything happens to Anita, hell will be raised around here. As it is, no one needs to know that she was ever taken. It's better if we keep all of that quiet for as long as possible.'

'They'll find out from Amos,' Florence said.

'No, I don't think so. I'm going to caution him against telling anyone why he took the money. Suggest that the kidnappers might come back and do more harm if he talks or if Anita ever identifies them.'

'Yes, that should work,' Florence agreed.

'But we must have the money! Didn't Earl Weathers ever tell you where he meant to take Anita?'

'He said it would be best if I didn't know. I might let something slip.'

Knowing Earl Weathers, Herb thought that the gunman had probably not told Florence because if he decided to take the money, leaving Anita behind, the girl would never be seen again. Without a victim, no one could convict him of kidnapping, a certain hanging offence. Herb

Pepper did not say this to Florence. Both of their heads turned toward the yard at the sound of an approaching team of horses. They stepped apart, Florence patting her hair as Herb seated himself to await the arrival of Amos Fillmore.

The two men's conversation didn't amount to much. In fact, after the marshal had left, Amos Fillmore found himself wondering why Pepper had bothered to ride all the way out there. The meeting was surprisingly terse and uninformative. Fillmore had hoped that the marshal had word concerning Anita, but he did not. They had already discussed the other matters Herb Pepper brought up: Fillmore was to tell no one that Anita had been taken, and not to worry about the bank's missing money.

'I'm hot on the trail of the kidnappers, Amos,' Pepper told him consolingly. 'I'll have that money back to you before the bank examiners have completed their investigation. After you replace it, they'll simply have to admit that they made a mistake. So long as you don't talk to anyone else, I can protect you.'

Laredo was also surprised by the shortness of the meeting. He had expected to have more time to poke around the area surrounding the Fillmore

House, but after Amos Fillmore's arrival, the marshal spent no more than five minutes talking to the banker. Laredo had followed Pepper out to the house to look for the kidnappers' sign Bill Thatcher had reported. He wanted to see it first-hand and draw his own conclusions.

He learned nothing new in his brief investigation. He did discover, however, that there was a connection between the banker and the local law. So Amos Fillmore had reported the kidnapping after all. But why would the two men choose to hold their meeting out here instead of in the marshal's office? To prevent the kidnappers from knowing that Fillmore, contrary to the kidnappers' instructions, had gone to the marshal? That seemed logical on the surface.

What bothered Laredo is that he had seen no sign that Pepper was doing any investigation on his own, nor had he shared any information he might have had with his deputy. Something was not right here.

At Herb Pepper's sudden reappearance from the house, Laredo heeled his horse and aimed it eastward, toward open desert, not wishing to be seen on the road back to Crater. He was just a little too slow. Through narrowed eyes, Herb Pepper watched the distant figure of a dark horseman riding from the Fillmore house, and he found himself worrying for the first time.

Someone was watching. But who? Soberly Herb Pepper swung heavily into the saddle and pointed his horse southward, toward Crater. Time was wasting. Pepper felt as if he was caught in a trap inside a trap. Damn Earl Weathers! Where was the gunman with their share of the money?

FIVE

Crater was in its late afternoon lull when Herb Pepper reached the town. The working folks had gone home and the drunks were not yet in full swing. Pepper rode his horse directly to the Long Trail Stable. Wink Rollins appeared wiping his hands on his greasy jeans, taking the reins to the marshal's bay mare.

'Everything all right?' the marshal asked.

'Fine, Marshal,' Wink said, but then he hesitated. 'There was one thing . . .'

'Tell me,' Pepper said, stretching his back.

'A stranger – he was eyeing my tooth pretty close,' Wink divulged. Pepper sighed heavily. There was always someone coveting Wink's gold tooth in Wink's mind. Still, the news of a stranger piqued Pepper's interest. Especially after spotting the mysterious rider at the Fillmores' place.

'What'd he look like?' Herb Pepper asked.

Wink described Laredo as well as he could, down to the staghorn-handled Colt he was wearing. He sounded like no one Pepper knew, but Wink hadn't finished yet.

'Wasn't long after he got here that he was in a scuffle,' Wink told the marshal. 'I seen him break up a fight between young Tad Becket and a couple of rowdies from the One Tree. Chased 'em off with his gun. Then he marched Tad over to your office.'

'Is that so?' Pepper asked, camouflaging his interest. 'Took Tad to report the assault, did he?'

'I wouldn't know about that, Marshal. I only know he and Tad went into your office and they were in there with Bill for quite awhile.'

'I'll ask Bill about it,' Pepper said easily. Damn right he would ask Bill Thatcher about it! The deputy had said nothing to him about some stranger getting involved in Tad's beating. He hadn't even mentioned the attack on the young teller.

Pepper's stomach growled. He was missing his evening steak dinner at Minnie's. Pepper had the idea that it might not be the last meal he missed for awhile. He stumped toward the jail in a sour mood.

The western sky was flaring with colour when Herb Pepper shouldered his way roughly into the marshal's office to find Bill Thatcher listlessly sweeping the floor. Bill turned mildly-surprised eyes toward him and paused in his work.

'Hello, Herb,' the deputy said.

'Sit down at my desk, Bill,' Pepper said, 'we have to talk.'

Bill leaned the broom in the corner and took a seat in the stiff-backed wooden chair facing the marshal who had lowered himself into his swivel chair. Pepper removed his hat, folded his thick hands together and said:

'Bill, we have to work together if this office is going to function properly.'

'Yes, sir,' Bill answered, struck by the marshal's hypocrisy. When had Pepper ever been interested in sharing information?

'This afternoon Tad Becket was assaulted,' Pepper went on. He managed to honestly look surprised. 'You said nothing to me. There was another man involved, a stranger. You didn't tell me about him either.'

'Tad got roughed up. It wasn't much,' Bill said defensively. 'The stranger – well, we have them passing through from time to time.'

'Yes, that's true enough, Bill. But just now, with

70

everything that's happening, it could be important.'

Bill pondered the marshal's words. With everything that was happening? Marshal Pepper had insisted that nothing was happening outside the usual. He doubted that Fillmore had taken money from the bank, he had not said a word about the possibility that Anita Fillmore had been kidnapped. Bill answered guardedly.

'What do you mean, Herb?'

'What do I mean?' Pepper's hands flew up excitedly. 'The bank examiners and all. Where are they anyway?'

'They've finished and left town,' Bill said calmly. Didn't Pepper know anything? Or did he know far more than Bill did?

'That was short work.'

'Maybe they didn't find anything,' Bill suggested.

'Or maybe they're off to file a complaint. They never even talked to me!' Pepper grumbled. No, they hadn't, and Bill Thatcher knew that this was because of his own warning message not to take the local law into their confidence.

Pepper sighed, placed both his meaty hands flat on his desktop and said, 'I want to know who this stranger is, Bill.'

There was no way of getting around it, Bill knew. Pepper's eyes were boring into him. He decided to tell the truth – or a part of it. 'His name is Laredo. He is from the Bank Examiner's office, too. Enforcement branch, he said. I guess it's his job to track down any missing money and arrest the thief.'

'He told you all of that?' Pepper said, annoyance deepening the flush on his broad face. 'And you said nothing to me.'

Bill Thatcher sat silently. He had no good answer for his silence concerning Laredo. He could hardly say that he didn't think it was important. He sat waiting for Pepper to lash him with his tongue, to scream, curse or pound the desk.

'Well,' Pepper said instead, his voice surprisingly mild, 'I'll want to talk to him. Do you know where he's staying?'

'No, I don't.'

'I'll find him.' Pepper was thinking of many things at once, his mind spiraling, hesitating, surging one direction and then another. Bill was unimportant now. This Laredo, though, he was important. What did he want? Did he know, or had he guessed about the link between the bank embezzlement and Anita Fillmore's kidnapping?

Was it Laredo that Pepper had seen earlier lurking near the Fillmore house? Did that mean – the marshal wondered in momentary panic – that Laredo's thinking had gotten so far that he now suspected a link between the theft and Marshal Pepper himself?

One certainty emerged from all of these tangled thoughts – Laredo had to be eliminated. Removed from the scene until Earl Weathers delivered a share of the bank's money to him. Assuming that the bastard had any intention of following through with his end of the deal. No matter, not for now. For now Pepper decided that he could only plan one step at a time.

The first step was to get rid of Laredo.

Laredo had returned to Crater and was stabling his chestnut at the Long Trail. Lantern light from low-burning lamps cast sketchy shadows around the interior of the stable. It was several minutes before Wink Rollins appeared out of the darkness of the horse-scented building. Wink started to smile, hid his tooth with his hand and said soberly:

'You planning on staying on in Crater?'

Laredo said, 'Yes I am, why?'

'Just wondering,' Wink said, taking the reins to the chestnut horse. 'Some men wouldn't wish to stay around here long.' If his cryptic remark was meant to convey a warning, it wasn't definite enough to do any more than cause Laredo to frown slightly. Still, it seemed, the cat was out of the bag – his presence in Crater was no longer a secret. He left the stable and stood watching the stars gather above the long desert, considering.

Perhaps he should step into one of the saloons and wait, hoping to catch Bill Thatcher making his evening rounds. Bill might have some new information that would help. He was hungry, too, very hungry he realized. He should find some small eatery where he could have a meal in peaceful anonymity. His stomach resolved the debate. Hunger was nagging at him strongly enough not to be longer ignored. He started back uptown, using the alleyways, avoiding the main street. In a strange town restaurants were the easiest places to find. The good smells of cooking needed no posted sign to announce them.

The night was still and warm. The loudest sound in the near-silence was the steady pacing of Laredo's boots.

They came out after him where the alley was its darkest.

Laredo saw the two figures of men in front of him, indistinct silhouettes near the head of the alley. There were times past when he would have paid them no mind, but his life as a tracker of men had made him more cautious. The last time he had been not quite wary enough he had ended up in bed for six weeks with a bullet in his hip.

Laredo did not halt nor slow his stride, but he was suddenly alert, vigilant. He was nearly sure now that he had heard the scuffling of boots behind him as well, and his frown deepened, his hand positioned itself near the butt of his Colt. The men he was approaching had not shifted their stance. They were not facing each other which would have been natural had they been two men talking in the dark, but stood braced, facing Laredo as he approached them.

The running steps behind Laredo caused him to duck and spin. As a club whipped past his ear, he drove his elbow up and back with all the strength he could muster. His attacker let out a great gasp as he was struck in the V between his ribs and he collapsed onto the oily earth of the alley.

The two men at the head of the alley had reacted immediately. One of them, pistol drawn, steadied himself for a shot. There was no mercy in Laredo at that moment. Hurling himself to one side, he drew his own Colt and the gun thundered in the night, its bullet hitting its mark cleanly. The gunman was turned half around by the impact. He threw one arm into the air like a wild signal and then doubled up.

The last man attacked Laredo with blind fury. Laredo had let him get too close while his attention was focused on the man with the gun, and a bulky body slammed heavily into him, driving Laredo against the wall of the neighboring building. His pistol flew free and Laredo felt a sharp fiery pain in his ribs. Bringing up a knee, he drove his attacker back two steps, then kicked him hard on the kneecap. The big man staggered away howling, but he was not through. Laredo braced himself for a second attack by the larger man. The reason for his attacker's courage became obvious when the thug Laredo had dropped earlier grabbed Laredo from behind, pinning his arms.

Laredo writhed in his grip and threw his head back with violence. Laredo's skull caught the man holding him on the nose and he cursed and staggered back just a little. It was enough. As the first man, limping from a broken kneecap moved in to finish the job, Laredo was able to rock back against his captor and kick out with both boots.

His feet caught the big man in the chest and he spun away, stuggling for breath. The man holding Laredo kicked him on his heel and let fly a fist that thudded flush on Laredo's ear, tearing it. The big man, showing surprising spirit re-entered the fight, aiming a deliberate fist at Laredo's jaw. The blow landed solidly despite his wild twisting and turning and Laredo saw hot stars flare up behind his eyes. They were going to get him after all, damnit!

Furious, Laredo struck out with knees and feet, elbows and fists, catching flesh here, bone there, but his assailants were also relentless in their attack and Laredo felt a heavy fist land on the hinge of his jaw and loosen his knees, and he sagged toward the earth as the two men pummeled him with wild blows, their breath coming in ragged gasps.

'Hear, what's going on! Stop that or I'll shoot!' Laredo heard a voice cry out. The voice was somehow familiar, but he could not put a face to it. He rested on his knees, head hanging as the men released him and with one last parting kick took to their heels and fled up the alley. As Laredo's defender approached, he looked up at the shadowy figure, nodded in gratitude, and keeled over onto his face, out cold.

'What were you trying to do?' she asked as she dabbed at Laredo's cut face with a soft cloth damp with warm water.

'It was more a matter of what they were trying to do,' Laredo said with a smile that hurt his mouth.

Dusty Donegall rose, smiling faintly, worriedly and went out into her kitchen to refill the basin with hotter water. 'I think you're going to need a few stitches in your ear.'

'All right,' Laredo said.

'You killed one of them, you know,' she called out to him. Laredo glanced that way, seeing her slender back and cascading Irish red hair.

'I thought so. What were you doing back there anyway?'

Dusty was returning with the basin which smelled now of carbolic. Seating herself beside the sofa where Laredo lay, she answered: 'I was shopping for shoes.'

'Heck of a place to do that.'

'I always use the alleys. On Main Street the drunks always call out at me.'

'Oh,' was all Laredo could think to reply. The water, now laced with carbolic stung his torn ear as Dusty dabbed at it, her lips pursed in concentration. Her little white dog sat on the floor, watching its mistress. Now and then the eager eyes of the animal would flash as if with appreciation and its plumed tail would wag.

Dusty placed the basin aside and rose again.

When she returned it was with a round wooden container which she placed on her lap as she sat. She removed a needle and thread. Laredo winced in unhappy anticipation.

'When I saw them beating you,' Dusty told him, 'I lowered my voice and shouted at them. They took to their heels quick enough.'

'Did you recognize any of them?' Laredo asked.

'It was too dark. Anyway, I hardly know any of the men in town by sight. Now be quiet and hold still. This will hurt.'

And it did. A lot. Puffing slightly with concentration Dusty stitched the tear in Laredo's ear while he forced himself to endure it without twitching or complaining. Only the little white dog seemed to enjoy the game.

'There,' Dusty said at last, placing the sewing box aside. 'You're stitched up about as well as I can do.'

'Thank you,' Laredo said. He tried sitting up then, and made it, but with accompanying dizziness. The movement also triggered a headache and he leaned forward, holding his throbbing head in his hands.

'Are you going to be all right?'

'Yes. I've been in worse shape.'

'If this is how you look when you win a fight . . .

maybe you ought to consider another kind of work,' Dusty said, neither seriously nor with mockery.

'Maybe. I'm not much good at anything else, though,' Laredo said, turning his head to glance at the redhead who sat quietly, her blue eyes shining with warmth.

'Rest,' Dusty said, and her hand rested briefly on his battered shoulder before she rose and went off to boil some coffee for the two of them. She hummed softly as she worked and after a few minutes the pleasing aroma of coffee began to fill the room. It was a clean, agreeable little room Laredo decided, looking around. Not too crammed with women's gee-gaws; it was a neat, efficient place like the woman who owned it. Laredo wondered how Bill Thatcher could believe that Dusty was a rattlebrained chatterbox. He had witnessed none of that in the redhead.

Dusty had just returned with a tray holding two small coffee cups with blue flowers painted on them when the storm of rapping began at the door. Laredo reached automatically for his holster, but found it empty. Dusty handed him his staghorn-handled Colt.

'I picked it up,' she said and Laredo nodding his thanks rose stiffly and gestured for Dusty to stand aside.

'Come on in,' Laredo said, drawing back the handle of his Colt as the door swung open. Bill Thatcher appeared in the doorway, his face drawn, his eyes darting nervously around the room.

'Bill!' Dusty said. Laredo smiled and holstered his Colt. Bill did not smile in return. He said in a dry voice:

'Laredo – I've come to arrest you. For murder.'

SIX

Breakfast was bacon, grits and biscuits. The view was that of a cramped, disordered room seen through iron bars. Sunlight slanted low through a high, narrow window. Laredo's head throbbed and his ribs ached. Only his stomach was pleased with the new day.

Bill Thatcher approached the jail cell, his face long, his manner apologetic. 'I know it's a hell of a way to treat you, Laredo, but they issued a warrant for you. I had to pick you up.'

'Who swore out the complaint?' Laredo asked, passing his tray out through the slit in the bars provided for that.

'A man named Rafer Kipsko. I never heard of him before, but he and another man swear that you shot and killed their friend last night.'

'Then Rafer Kipsko was one of the men who

waylaid me. There was no one else around.'

'I suppose so,' Bill said. He stood facing Laredo, tray in his hands for a long minute before turning away. He placed the tray down on the marshal's desk and seated himself. 'They'll never hold you, Laredo. Marshal Pepper will have to release you in a few days.'

'That's all the time they need, isn't it?' Laredo asked laconically. He returned to the bunk which hung on iron chains from the cell wall, lay down and looked up at the high window.

'The kidnappers, you mean?'

'Them. They have the money now. They can take their time and just take a leisurely ride out of the territory – with or without Anita.'

'Surely they'll set her free!' Bill said with a surge of panic. Laredo was not smiling when he asked:

'Why would they? Why turn a potential witness loose?'

'Because . . .' Bill Thatcher fell off into bitter reflection. After a minute he said, 'I would never have arrested you, Laredo. I know it's all a frame. But it was my job! I'm a sworn lawman.'

'Nobody's blaming you,' Laredo said, speaking with his eyes closed. After awhile he added quietly, 'We should be out there now trying to track those men down.'

Bill didn't answer. He was fingering the deputy marshal's badge that was pinned to the front of his red shirt. Laredo seemed have fallen asleep, although Bill did not understand how he could have. *Anita!* He thought he was failing her: doing nothing but standing guard over a man he knew to be innocent, the one man willing to help him in his search. There is duty, he thought.

And then there is duty.

Laredo opened an eye at the sound of the growled curse from Bill Thatcher, the jingle of heavy keys on a key ring. Glancing that way, he saw Bill slap his badge down on the desk and turn toward the jail cell.

'You'll get yourself in a lot of trouble,' Laredo warned the young man.

'I don't care. I resign. It's the job or Anita. That's no choice at all. Are you ready to ride, Laredo?'

Marshal Herb Pepper sat at the back of the Tooth & Claw Saloon at a small round table. With him were Rafer Kipso and Torn Fallo, two of the men he had sent to teach Laredo a lesson. The third, Avery Pittman could not attend: Laredo had shot the man dead in the alley.

'You didn't tell us what kind of catamount you were sending us after,' Kipso, a broad-shouldered man with the face of an ape was saying, signaling to the bartender. There were very few men in the saloon at this hour and so the bartender was able to supply them with a fresh pitcher of beer almost immediately. When the aproned man had returned to his chores, Pepper growled at Kipso.

'There were three of you, damnit. Three against one. How could you come out on the losing end?'

'The man could shoot and he could fight,' said Tom Fallon whose nose was swollen to twice its normal size due to Laredo's head butt. 'Who was he, anyway?'

'Just some drifting troublemaker,' Pepper said, taking a swallow of beer.

'I hope he keeps on drifting,' Kipso said bitterly. 'I can hardly walk on this knee of mine. We're not going to have to show up in court are we, Herb?'

'No, no,' Herb Pepper said, waving a hand. 'I'll drop the charges in a day or so. I just wanted to teach the man a lesson. He can't get away with gunplay in my town.' Pepper sipped at his beer again and, wiping his mouth with the back of his hand said, 'I've got another chore that might interest you boys. There's good money in it.'

'No,' big Rafer Kipso said, pushing away from the table. 'Not for me. Ask some of the boys over at the One Tree. I've had my fill of trying to make easy money.'

It took Herb Pepper no more than an hour to find three men who were willing to ride with him. It took no more than a bottle of whiskey each and twenty dollars to boot to convince these 'special deputies' to assist him. Herb Pepper was not in the mood for riding, he didn't relish hitting the trail with three rough men whom he barely knew, but the time had come.

Earl Weathers had gone too far. Whatever trick the gunman was trying to pull, he needed to be reined in now and to have the rules of the game explained to him quite loudly and clearly. The kidnappers had not been heard from since Amos Fillmore had paid them off. Earl Weathers appeared to have his mind set on keeping all the ransom. The money was Pepper's. His and Florence Fillmore's. They were the ones who had designed the plan. Weathers and his two half-smart cronies had only been necessary tools.

Pepper wished that Florence had been more patient, waited to find a man more trustworthy than Earl Weathers, a man who was known to have a reckless background. Herb Pepper had believed that his own position as marshal would be enough to keep the man in check. After all, he had the right to arrest Weathers – or gun him down if that was necessary.

And it seemed that it might have become necessary.

Marshal Pepper made his way slowly toward the Long Trail Stable. The day was clear again, the sky white, the sun brutally hot. Pepper wished that he had not spent the morning drinking with Crater's low element. His head had begun to ache just behind his eyes. The musty, shaded interior of the stable was welcome relief. Pepper called out for Wink Rollins and the narrow man with the single gold tooth emerged from a shadowy corner to greet him.

'Be needing your mare?' Wink asked.

'That's why I'm here,' Pepper growled. His mood was not improving. All he had to look forward to on this day was a long wearying ride across the desert flats, searching for that coyote, Earl Weathers.

'Going to be a busy day?' Wink Rollins asked in a drawl as he slipped the marshal's bridle from the nail on the wall where it had been hanging.

'Yes,' Pepper answered.

'Thought so. Thought so when Bill Thatcher took his horse out,' Wink said slyly, 'his and the other man's.'

'What other man?' Pepper demanded, suddenly alert.

'The stranger – the one that was riding the big chestnut horse. The man you locked up for shooting Avery Pittman.'

Pepper felt his heart rate increase. He shouted at Wink: 'Bill had the stranger with him!'

'No, marshal,' Wink said carefully, 'but he took the man's horse.'

'Saddle my mare,' Pepper ordered. 'I'll be right back.'

Stamping into the marshal's office, Herb Pepper saw, as he had half-expected, that the cell where they had been holding Laredo was empty and that the door had swung wide open. And on his desk, a stray beam of light from the high window glinted on Bill Thatcher's badge. Pepper cursed, removed a Winchester from the gunrack, a box of shells from the desk drawer and took a few deep, calming breaths.

Maybe this would all work out for the best. They would now have six men in the hunt for the girl and the money. For certainly that was what Bill Thatcher had in mind – finding the girl. If Bill and the stranger, Laredo, were able to track down Earl Weathers, Trotter and Morris, why then it was fine. If there was any trouble with them later, why

Pepper would explain that Laredo was an escaped prisoner wanted for murder, and Bill . . . well, he had removed his badge and freed the stranger. If they were caught with the money, it would be a simple matter to convince people that they had been trying to make their own run for it, and when they had fired on Pepper and his posse, the marshal had had no choice but to shoot back.

Too bad if Bill and the stranger both happened to be killed.

Yes, Pepper thought as he went out, closing the door heavily behind him, things weren't as desperate as they had looked at first glance. In fact, Bill Thatcher was going to make this all easier for him.

As for the girl – Pepper's thinking hadn't gotten that far. It all depended on what Anita witnessed, where she was found. It would be a shame if something happened to her, but if it came down to it, Anita Fillmore might just have to be done away with as well. That, too, could be explained away later. It would be believed that the crazy Earl Weathers had killed her. There would be no one left alive to contradict the marshal's version of events.

Pepper's headache had abated. Now, squinting into the bright sun, he made his way back to the stable, his spirits higher than they had been only minutes earlier.

'Why don't you just take your bottle and go?' Ruben Dryer was suggesting strongly to the narrow man who was half sprawled across the back table at the Tooth & Claw Saloon. Dryer was bartender there, and more than used to trouble. He was also used to men who were a plain nuisance like Ike Morris, the drunk man he was speaking to.

'Not my turn yet,' Ike said without lifting his head.

'You're wrong,' Dryer said shaking Ike's shoulder. 'It is your turn. Your turn to walk on out of here. Or do I have to get the marshal?'

'No!' Ike said, suddenly coming alert. He pawed at his red eyes and attempted a smile. 'I'll be on my way, Ruben. You say I've got a bottle I can take?'

'You paid for one when you came in. Said you wanted to make sure you had one to travel on before you drank up the rest of your money.' Ruben Dryer wondered where a dedicated drunk like Ike was getting his money these days, but it was not considered good form to ask such questions in Crater.

'All right,' Ike said, struggling to his feet. 'I'm on my way. Gimme the bottle.'

Dryer recovered the bottle he had wrapped in brown paper from behind the bar and handed it to Ike Morris who took it with a shaking hand and staggered out into the harsh glare of the day.

There were a few scattered ponds along Thorne Creek, although the flow of the water had ceased more than a month ago. At one of these ponds, in the scattered shade of a flourishing cottonwood tree, Bill Thatcher and Laredo watered their horses.

'It was just about here that I lost the kidnappers' trail,' Bill was saying, pointing across the sandy expanse of Thorne Creek. 'I followed them up among those rocks and had the sign vanish on me.'

'They were heading toward higher ground,' Laredo commented, squinting into the sunlight toward the low broken hills beyond. They were a gray, patternless mass of disconnected ranges cut by narrow crooked canyons. Nothing much grew there – some sage, Spanish bayonet and a wide variety of cactus.

'Well, it makes sense,' Bill was forced to agree. 'They could keep a close watch on their backtrail if they were up in the hills somewhere, but there's not much up there. I mean, no ranches or working mines.'

'Were there ever?' Laredo asked with interest.

'Once a few folks tried for silver, but they mostly came up broke and disappointed. There's only one real strike in this area.' Bill pointed eastward, 'The Cummins Company runs that.'

'Yes,' Laredo said, still studying the northern hills. 'But I guess a lot of people have looked for silver up there.'

'Dozens,' Bill replied. 'Now and then we still have men who come in to purchase mining supplies. They will go up into the hills, scratch around for a few months, dig exploratory shafts and return home, tails dragging.'

'No ranches, no towns, but hundreds of caves and tunnels,' Laredo commented, glancing at Bill.

'You think Earl Weathers is holed up in an abandoned mine.'

'It make sense, doesn't it? Does Weathers know the country hereabouts?'

'I don't think so,' Bill said removing his hat to mop at his perspiring forehead, 'but Kyle Trotter does. Before he went to work for the Fillmore family, he was among those wandering miners.'

'Is that so,' Laredo said. Kyle Trotter, then, had not only worked for Amos Fillmore but was familiar with the multitude of mine shafts dotting the rugged hills.

'You're pretty sure, aren't you?' Bill asked, gathering up the reins to his piebald horse.

'Aren't you? It only makes sense.'

'But,' Bill said, sighing with exasperation, 'as I told you, there must be a hundred old mines up there. How could we ever find the right one? Assuming that the kidnappers are still there.'

'I don't know,' Laredo said, swinging into the saddle of his chestnut horse, 'but having a look beats what we're doing here.' Maybe, he was thinking, they could again cut the kidnappers' sign although the tracks were now almost four days old. Slim chance, but the area was little-travelled and there had been no rain to erase the signs of their passing.

They could do no more than try.

Starting their horses down into the sandy wash, they crossed it and rode up the greasewood-stippled far bank, heading north. The hours passed in slow, dull progression. The heat became stultifying; no breeze stirred across the desert expanse. The sun on their backs was blistering. Their mouths remained dry no matter how often they sipped water from their canteens. The hills seemed to draw no nearer as morning merged with afternoon. The ride was long. How long had it seemed to Anita, bound, not knowing where she was heading or what her fate might be?

Laredo's hand was thrust out suddenly, touching Bill's elbow.

'What is it?' the deputy asked.

'Look to your right, back a quarter mile or so.'

Bill let his eyes scour the empty desert. Nothing. Then through the distorting veils of heat, he saw, or thought he saw, a lone rider heading north. The man was tracking away from them, riding slightly more eastward.

'Wonder where he's going,' Bill said. There was no normal trail in that direction, no known destination.

'I think we'd better find out,' Laredo said in a low voice. 'We don't have any idea where we're going – that man seems to have a goal in mind.'

'Do you think he's one of the kidnappers?' Bill asked excitedly.

'I think he knows where he's going, that's all,' Laredo answered. 'Let's see if it's the same place we want to go.'

It was little more than a hunch that sent them riding in the direction of the lone rider, but the desert was lightly travelled, and a man out here alone must have some particular aim in mind. This was no idle wanderer. They followed after him.

Within an hour they had closed the distance on

the rider who evinced no interest in moving faster than at his steady indifferent pace. Laredo and Bill briefly lost sight of the man as they approached a low, rocky knoll. They were now nearly in the shadows of the jagged hills and the land began to thrust up here and there, folding on itself. Cresting the knoll they paused to reorient themselves. The rider was not more than fifty yards off and Laredo heard Bill murmur something harshly to himself.

'What?' Laredo prompted.

'I think I know who that is. He doesn't belong out here.' At Laredo's questioning glance, Bill told him, 'It's Ike Morris. He's a stone drunkard. He won't be found more than a dozen steps from the nearest bottle. Why would he be riding the desert?'

Even as Bill was explaining, Laredo saw the horseman lift something to his lips. Sunlight glinted on glass. It seemed that Bill was correct in naming his man.

'Ike Morris,' Bill mused. 'What in hell would bring him out here?'

'Have you seen him around town lately?' Laredo asked. 'You make the rounds of the saloons every night, don't you?'

'Yes I do,' Bill replied. 'And no, no I haven't seen Ike around lately now that you ask. Had I noticed his absence, I would just have thought that he'd finally drunk himself to death. He's not the sort of man you pay much attention to.'

'Until now,' Laredo said. 'Now, I think we are going to have to pay close attention to him.' Everything Bill had said was little more than conjecture, but there was no reasonable explanation for such a man to be riding alone into the open desert.

Unless he had friends out here.

'Let him get a little farther ahead,' Laredo said when Bill wanted to start his horse forward. 'We can't risk spooking him now.'

They rode on in silence, crossing the sun-bright empty land, the tangle of broken hills, following the little man who might hold the key to the missing bank money's location and knowledge of Anita Fillmore's fate.

Marshal Herb Pepper cursed again and shifted again heavily in the saddle. Between the ears of his bay mare he watched as the endless, rock-strewn desert passed. The pale sky was hot, airless; the silver sun lashed at their shoulders and backs with unabating torment. Pepper glanced only now and then at his 'special deputies' who lagged behind him, silent and sullen. Men who spent the better part of their days holed up in saloons were not experienced trailsmen. Yes, they had accepted the offer of cash money and whiskey quickly enough; it was when they had to repay that they faltered and fell into dark discontent. Pepper could feel their malevolent eyes his back. They were like a pack of dogs that had been dragged from the kennel for some unknown and unwelcome task.

Pepper thought that had he waited until evening when more men were about he might have found more competent and willing riders. But by then the land would be growing too dark for tracking and the available men drunker still. In an emergency a man does what he must, even if that involves hiring malcontents like the brutish Pastor Cobb and the surly MacGowan brothers.

Cobb had one eye which protruded more than the other in his beefy face and kinky grey hair that straggled down his neck. Under his hat, Pepper knew, was a bald, flattened skull. Cobb was a fighting man, but he was unused to discipline and nearly impossible to convince with logic.

The MacGowan brothers were a mystery. They were slight, pale blond, green-eyed and usually similarly attired in jeans and plaid shirts. Their given names were Robert and Anchor, although Pepper didn't know which was which – it had never seemed important – but he thought Anchor was slightly taller, Bob the left-handed one. They had ridden into Crater a month earlier from Texas, seated themselves at the One Tree Saloon's bar and stayed there. Most of their time was spent staring into space. Occasionally they would burst into wild laughter at some comment passed only between the two of them. They had made no friends. They had never cut up badly enough to get themselves arrested. They wore their Colt revolvers as if they knew what they were for.

All in all this was the sorriest posse Pepper had ever formed. No matter – if they fought when they were told to, they would do. It would all work out.

So long as these three unpredictable misfits did not find out how much money was involved. They had been told only that Bill Thatcher had released a murderer and was on the run with him for unknown reasons, and that it was these two men the posse was pursuing. That much was true, but when the others – especially Pastor Cobb – listened to the story, Pepper saw shadows of doubt in their eyes. Perhaps, the marshal thought, they knew him too well, knew that it would take more than what Thatcher and Laredo had done to prompt him to ride out onto the long desert in the summer heat.

It did not matter what these three thought. Earl

Weathers was out here somewhere, and the money. One last difficult trek and it would all come to an end, Pepper was thinking. From here on his life would be only comfort and ease. He and Florence living it up in some big city hotel. All he had to do was hold this posse together long enough to track down that cheating Earl Weathers. Then it would be at an end. The long ride would be well worth it once the dog, Weathers, was lying on the desert floor and the ransom was safe in the marshal's saddle-bags.

SEVEN

'I still don't see them,' Kyle Trotter said, turning from the mouth of the shallow cave to look back to where Anita Fillmore sat dismally against the wall of the cleft that the silver-hunters had quarried into the stone. Her eyes were hidden in dark circles after nearly four days of captivity. Dirt streaked her face, showing traces of tear rivulets. Her long blond hair was an untidy tangle. Her lips were slightly parted as if she would say something, but she remained silent.

'What do you think could have happened?' Kyle Trotter asked in the way he had that made it unclear if he was talking to Anita or to himself. He had been standing at the entrance to the cave staring out at the glitter of the long desert for nearly half an hour, hoping, expecting to see Earl

Weathers returning or Ike Morris arriving for his turn to stand guard over Anita.

'Ike, you can figure he got drunk – fell off his horse or got himself arrested,' Kyle Trotter continued, his eyes on Anita's. 'But Earl! What could have happened to him? He said he'd be back shortly, and you can take Earl Weathers' word.'

'When that much money's involved?' Anita asked suggestively. She had tried from time to time to sow mistrust among the kidnappers, thinking that she might somehow use it to her advantage. Normally the men paid no attention to her. Now Kyle Trotter seemed to give her question some thought.

The fat man's eyebrows drew together. His fingers tapped rhythmically against the butt of his holstered pistol. For the first time Anita thought Trotter's face reflected concern. His frown held for a long minute, but then Trotter laughed and shook his head.

'Earl Weathers! You never have to worry about that man once his word is given,' Trotter said. He wandered again to the front of the cave, his bulky body silhouetted by the brilliant sunlight beyond. He laughed again and lifted a stubby, pointing finger.

101

'Look at me!' he said, 'Worried about nothing. Here comes Ike now. I recognize that paint pony he rides.'

Anita accepted this information without interest. These two would make no decision about her destiny. That was in Earl Weathers' hands. As far as changing guards went, it made very little difference to her. True, Kyle Trotter sometimes loosened her bonds for a while, but then he began talking incessantly about his apparently empty past. Ike usually stayed awake until Kyle had turned in and fallen asleep then simply drank until he passed out leaving her alone in the dark silence wine company of the rustling things that lived in the cavern depths. Anita was not sure whether she preferred the hours she was forced to endure Trotter's endless rambling or the deadly silence of Ike Morris' midnight watch.

If only she could free herself. She had wished, hoped, that Kyle Trotter would forget to re-tie her bonds, leave her alone in the night with the sleeping Ike Morris, but he never did. Where she would go, Anita did not know, but a stumbling, directionless run across the open desert seemed as welcome as the open doors to paradise.

There was a faint reddish glow to the sky when Ike Morris finally made his appearance. Weaving his way into the cave, the bulge formed by the whiskey bottle in his coat pocket obvious. Anita thought that Kyle Trotter looked barely able to keep himself in check, to avoid giving Ike a dressing down. Trotter said nothing, however. He was apparently resigned to the drunken Ike Morris' behaviour. There was no point in trying to change the man now, or trying to shame him.

'Where's Earl?' Ike asked, searching the darkness of the cave with blood-red eyes.

'That's what I was going to ask you,' the fat man said. 'He's not here, hasn't been here all day.'

The two men showed different reactions to the absence of Earl. Trotter continued to fret and returned to the mouth of the cave to stare out at the desert, which was colouring with the last light of day. Ike Morris took Earl's absence as a signal to open his bottle again and to drink freely.

'Mr Trotter,' Anita said in a dry voice. 'These knots are cutting off my circulation again. And I could use a drink of water, if you please.'

Trotter turned, glanced at Ike who had seated himself at the dilapidated table, head on his forearms, and sighed. He crossed the cave, worried about and alternately angry with the missing Earl Weathers. He loosened Anita's bonds as she had requested. He wished nothing ill for

Anita Fillmore, although the matter was beyond his control. He had worked for the Fillmores, had befriended, or attempted to befriend Anita while he worked around the property. She was attractive, bright, active. Or she had been. Now she was a downcast prisoner. He rose, smiling dully at Anita and walked to where three canteens rested on the stone floor of the cave. Now he did growl at Ike Morris, 'This is supposed to be your turn to watch,' but Ike did not so much as twitch a muscle.

Muttering under his breath Trotter returned to where Anita sat. He knelt, allowing her to drink water from the tin cup he held to her lips.

Where in hell was Earl Weathers? Trotter thought. They had gotten the money, by now they should be on the long trail, riding as far as possible from Crater. Trotter considered, had to consider, that Earl had ridden away with the money himself, but he could not allow himself to believe that, as apparent as it was becoming. If that were so, all of this had been for nothing and it would be up to Kyle Trotter himself what to do with Anita.

Anita, finished sipping at the water, cocked her head and let her eyes narrow. 'Do I hear someone coming?' she asked, and Trotter jumped to his feet and rushed toward the mouth of the cave. He stood half bent forward, peering into the settling darkness.

As he did Anita managed to slip one loop of the restraining rope free and conceal it in her palms.

'I don't see no one,' Trotter mumbled and returned to Anita. With his eyes still on the cave opening he tightened the knot on the rope circling Anita's chafed wrists. Anita's heart raced; she held her breath fearfully, but Trotter did not notice that one loop of hemp had been slipped free and was now hidden between Anita's hands. The rope now had a good six to eight inches of slack in it. Anita thought she could slip her hands free without difficulty. And then she would. . . .

But there was no 'and then', she had no idea what she might be able to do next.

She sat silently, watching as the sky grew dark, watching Kyle Trotter strike a match and light the wick of the lantern. He shook Ike Morris's shoulder roughly, enough to cause Ike to sit up momentarily, and then Trotter made for his blankets in the corner.

He rolled up in the uncomfortable bed he had made, kicked at his blankets and pulled his hat over his eyes, somehow falling asleep as Anita sat silently watching the flickering lamplight, the distant silver stars and Ike Morris whose head began to sag until eventually he was in a deep sleep, sitting up but unconscious to the world, his bristled chin resting on his chest. The lantern burned more dully. Anita slipped the rope on her wrists and with frantic energy went to work on the twisted hemp binding her ankles.

Kyle Trotter snored sharply. Ike Morris grunted a drunken response. Anita painfully tore a fingernail on the knots, but worked on with wild determination, her eyes on her two captors.

Free at last, she tried to tuck her legs under her and rise, but she could not move them! Her lower extremities were paralyzed by a lack of circulation, and she kneaded at the calves of her legs and ankles frantically. The circulation returned rapidly, but painfully. Her legs and feet felt as if they were being pricked by thousands of needles. Anita had to bite her lip to keep herself from crying out.

Long minutes passed. When she thought that she could make it, she tried again, tucking her legs under and trying to stand. Her legs refused her, though. In a panic she began crawling forward across the rough floor of the stone chamber. Ike Morris twitched, and he scratched at his whiskered jaw. His red eyes flickered open, but his gaze was unfocused. When his eyes closed again, Anita went on, scooting, crawling, clawing at the cavern floor until somehow she was out of the mouth of the stony shaft, fresh desert air sweeping over her body, brushing her long hair across her face.

She struggled to her feet and started on her way, hobbling, stumbling towards the wild desert nightscape below her.

'What are they doing?' Bill Thatcher asked in a whisper. Laredo was higher up on the cactus-stippled knoll, and he was able to look down to where Marshal Herb Pepper's ragtag posse had halted.

'They've lost our tracks,' Laredo whispered back. 'They're making night camp.'

'What do we do now?'

'Keep moving,' Laredo said, slipping back down the knoll. 'Put some space between us and them. Just keep it silent.'

Bill nodded dismally. He was out of his depth now, and he knew it. Maybe he wasn't much of a lawman anyway, but he and the town of Crater had reached an uneasy understanding. He did his duty as required and no more. In some respects maybe he was not much better than Pepper when it came to that. The situation they had now ridden into was far more complicated and much deadlier than rousting a few bar-room drunks. Bill knew that he would have to place his trust in Laredo's instincts.

The two men Indianed their way back to where their weary horses stood ground-hitched, slipped into leather and started at a walking pace up the long rocky ravine.

Emerging from the draw, they found themselves within a few hundred yards of the bulky hills. The faces of the surrounding cliffs were bleached by the faint light of the rising crescent moon.

'We'll never find what we're looking for, not in this light,' Bill said, still throttling his voice to a whisper.

'No,' Laredo agreed. They had made as much progress as possible on this night. He was about to tell Bill to swing down from his horse again when a movement to the east caught his eyes. Laredo reached for his rifle scabbard and then halted his movement. He could only stare at the apparition approaching them.

In a white robe, its movements faltering and awkward, the creature made its staggering approach. Now its arms went up and they heard a hoarse cry emerge from its throat before it fell.

'Anita!' Bill yelled, throwing caution aside, and heeled his piebald horse roughly, sending it pounding across the rocky ground toward the motionless woman who lay, a white, moon-lit, shapeless creature against the grey stone.

By the time Laredo caught up with them, Bill had dismounted recklessly and rushed to Anita Fillmore, lifting her to a seated position. Her face was as pale as the moon; her feet, Laredo saw were bruised and torn, the blood appearing like black ribbons in this light.

Her eyes were open; her expression was feverish, but she managed to lift one hand and place it against Bill Thatcher's cheek. 'I knew you would come for me,' she managed to say.

Laredo had unlooped the strap of his canteen from his saddlehorn, and now he joined them, handing Bill the canteen. Anita looked at Laredo, frowned with puzzlement and returned her gaze to Bill Thatcher who was petting her head, shushing her and trying to give her a drink of water while he himself seemed ready to break into sobs. Laredo watched them for a moment and then turned his eyes toward their backtrail. Who knew if Pepper and his men had heard something.

Who knew if the Earl Weathers gang was pursuing the girl?

Laredo spoke to Anita. 'Where's the money, Miss Fillmore? Who's got it?'

Her words came slowly but distinctly. 'It's not up there. Earl Weathers took off with the ransom. The two men he left behind don't know where he is.'

Bill was still stroking Anita's head, still murmuring to her. Laredo felt that he was as romantic as anyone, but he told them gruffly, 'We've got to get out of here. Pepper's not far off.'

'Marshal Pepper?' Anita asked, perplexed by Laredo's warning.

'I'll explain later,' Bill promised, and the girl only nodded her head as Thatcher helped her to her feet where she stood shakily, in obvious discomfort. Laredo stood apart, frowning. He had convinced himself that they were nearly within reach of the stolen bank money. Now, it seemed, the gunman Weathers had ridden off with it, abandoning his two cohorts and Anita. And where would Weathers ride? There was no telling. It was a long and uncompromising desert. Laredo felt the dull pangs of failure settling in his stomach.

He had failed once more. Weathers had several days lead on him, and all of the resources in the world. He turned to Bill and said roughly:

'Get her back to Crater.'

'I want to go home,' Anita said weakly. She was seated in front of Bill Thatcher now on the piebald pony's back. Her head lolled on her neck. She had used all of the strength she possessed just making it this far.

'I'll take her home instead,' Bill told Laredo.

'No,' Laredo said firmly. He had not given up the idea that the kidnapping scheme was a put-up job, that the banker himself might have fallen in with Weathers to formulate it. Where was Earl Weathers? There was no telling, but Laredo thought it was possible that he was sitting in Amos Fillmore's parlor, the two laughing at the way they had tricked everyone. He had to be sure.

'Take her to Dusty's. She'll be safe there,' Laredo ordered.

'But Laredo. . . .' Bill started to object, but Laredo snapped out at him again.

'Do it!'

'It's all right, Bill. I don't mind going to Dusty's,' Anita said. Those were the last words Laredo heard either of them say as he swung onto his chestnut's back, jerked the reins and started the big horse westward.

'Pepper, wake up,' Pastor Cobb whispered, shaking the marshal's shoulder roughly. Pepper woke up to squint at the pop-eyed man, the haze of starlit sky beyond him.

'What the hell do you want?' Pepper asked threateningly.

'I heard horses moving,' Cobb said. 'Not far off.

Better get up.'

Shaking off the heavy sleep, the result of hours of unaccustomed riding, Pepper managed to find his boots and tug them on. Cobb was standing in the darkness, peering northward toward the scattered hills, Anchor and Bob MacGowan were also rising from their beds. After Pepper had reached his feet, Cobb told him:

'There's something else, Marshal. I walked up to the hills. It was so faint I wasn't sure at first – but there's some kind of light burning halfway up one of those hills.'

'What are you talking about?' Pepper said, still angry. He tucked his shirt in as the brutish Cobb answered.

'Either a low fire or a lantern, maybe. Burning right up on the hillside. Must be someone in one of those caves up there.'

Pepper shrugged away his annoyance. If Cobb was right then perhaps they had found the kidnappers' hideout, the missing money. He had revealed none of this to Cobb and the MacGowan brothers. They still believed that they were chasing Thatcher and Laredo, and they were eagerly anticipating the reward Pepper had promised them should they track down the deputy and the escaped man.

Pepper buckled on his gunbelt and looked across the moon-shadowed desert toward the hills. He could not see the light Cobb claimed to have seen, but he trusted the man's skill if not his character. 'Saddle up, men,' Pepper said, 'let's have us a look.'

Something had awakened Kyle Trotter and he sat up in his blankets with an aching back and a sour taste in his mouth. He glanced at Ike Morris, passed out drunk at the table. Ike was snoring heavily, but that was not what Kyle had heard. He was used to the liquored-up snoring of Ike by now. Looking to the back of the cave, Trotter's heart jumped. There was a pile of ropes there, but no Anita Fillmore. The fool Ike Morris had let the girl slip right past him in the night.

Trotter grabbed for his pistol, stormed to where Ike sat sagged against the table and pounded his back and shoulders with his fist.

'Wake up you drunken fool! The girl's gone. Earl will have us for breakfast.' Even as he said that, Kyle Trotter reflected that he had long lost any hope that Earl Weathers would return with their share of the bank money. Four days was a long time. The gun fighter was probably in Mexico, laughing at their stupidity.

'What, who?' Ike rose to his feet, muttering, reaching for the empty whiskey bottle. Kyle Trotter started toward the mouth of the cave, wondering how much of a chance they had in running the girl down. The moon, slender as it was, had risen and they still had their horses. There was a chance, and they needed to take it. If the girl made it back to Crater and reported them, it would be the same as issuing death warrants for Ike and Kyle Trotter.

Kyle glanced back at Ike who was fumbling his sidearm on and then looked back to the desert. It was only then that he realized that the sounds that had awakened him had not been made by Anita's escape.

There were four horsemen approaching the cave. Kyle muttered a bitter oath and raced towards the lantern, blowing it out, though that would do them little good if the tracking men had already located their hideout.

Four days. Kyle had known better. A hunted man can only stay in one place for so long before by skill or chance the pursuers find him. Now they were in a tight spot. Their horses were too far away for them to make a break for them. Kyle found himself pinned in a cave with only a drunken fool to side him in a fight. There was, however, no choice. They would make a fight of it.

Herb Pepper and his posse had dismounted once more. The light they had been following had been extinguished, but they had their target located and it remained visible in the feeble glow of the light cast by the crescent moon. Pastor Cobb touched Pepper's elbow and jabbed a pointing finger upslope. Looking that way Pepper too could make out the silhouettes of two horses, their heads lifted alertly.

'Looks like we got 'em,' Cobb said. Pepper nodded. It looked like it, but who had they found?

They split. Herb Pepper and Cobb waited while the MacGowan brothers slipped away in the darkness to approach the cave from the opposite side, cutting off any escape route. They allowed the MacGowans fifteen minutes and then began their own ascent towards the small black hole bored into the face of the hill, pistols drawn. Pepper was grim, his stomach knotted with the tension of the moment. He did not know himself if it was Bill Thatcher and Laredo they had cornered or part of Earl Weathers' gang. One thing he did know for certain—

There would be bloodshed on this night.

EIGHT

Ike Morris stood trembling in the night. The temperature inside the cave remained warm. The chill he felt came from within. He needed a drink! With his heavy Colt in hand he stood beside the cavern mouth staring down at the desert which appeared as blurred shadows and incomplete forms to his bleary vision. The crash from behind him caused his head to jerk that way. Kyle Trotter had turned the table over to provide a flimsy bulwark. Ike looked doubtfully at the dilapidated table.

'That won't stop any .44 bullet, Kyle.'

'Shut up,' Kyle Trotter answered. He knew that Ike was right, but Kyle was not fighting with his mind now, but with his guts which were writhing, twisting and turning, sending a message to his brain that they wanted to survive this night.

'Maybe we should just give up,' Ike said dismally.

'Sure, why not?' Kyle mocked. 'Then we'll just see how long it takes them to string us up for kidnapping the girl.'

'Maybe they don't even know who we are. Maybe they're just passing strangers, maybe. . . .'

The first bullet, fired from below, caught Ike Morris in the skull, just above his ear and sent him to the floor of the cave like a sandbag dropping. His pistol clattered free. Kyle Trotter hunkered town behind the scant security of the upturned table, his thumb ratcheting back the hammer of his Colt revolver.

He expected the men – whoever they were – to approach cautiously, but they were suddenly there clotting the cave mouth, guns filling the darkness with flame and smoke and ricocheting lead. Kyle felt a bullet fired through the table tag his side just below the last rib and in frantic anger he shot back four times. One of his bullets caught a popeyed man in the chest and he staggered back, his pistol firing into the ceiling. A second man, a blond holding his pistol in his left hand, caught a .44 slug from Kyle's gun, opened his mouth as if to speak and fell forward, dying before he hit the stone floor.

Herb Pepper looked left and right frantically, seeing two of his posse shot and probably killed by the man behind the table and he emptied his revolver into the old wood, blowing it to fragments. He reloaded with shaky fingers as Anchor MacGowan crept nearer, his eyes wide with caution. Anchor stepped over the still form of his brother, raised his pistol higher and kicked the table aside. Kyle Trotter, shot to ribbons, lay behind the table, his gray shirt blood-splotched, pistol still in his hand. Somehow he was still breathing as Pepper approached him, toed the pistol out of Kyle's limp fingers and demanded:

'Where's the money?' He had no reason to expect Kyle Trotter to answer, but the dying man's lips moved and he said:

'Earl . . . took it and left us for dead meat.' Then the man died, his eyes remaining open reflecting a sort of dull confusion.

Anchor MacGowan was at Herb Pepper's shoulder when the dying man took his last breath. The blond gunman was frowning. The re-lighted lantern had already allowed him to see the coil of knotted ropes lying on the floor of the cave. Anchor began to reassess matters. He had hired on to track down a fugitive and his rogue deputy pal, but it was obvious now that the marshal had another agenda.

'What money's he talking about?' Anchor asked quietly, his finger on the trigger of his cocked revolver. Pepper turned to face him.

Wearing a smile, the marshal said, 'Why that money of course,' and he pointed toward the corner of the cave.

When Anchor turned his head that way Pepper shot him in the back, the bullet tagging Anchor MacGowan's heart.

As the smoke from his weapon settled, Pepper looked around the cave, seeing nothing but the carnage. It was true – Earl Weathers had taken off with the money. How had the girl gotten free? Had someone rescued her or were these two fools Weathers had left behind to watch her simply neglectful? It was of no importance.

Weathers was. He had the bank loot – his own share and the share that rightly belonged to Pepper and Florence. The money the two of them intended to use to start a new life for themselves, far away from Crater and Amos Fillmore. Pepper walked to the mouth of the cave, holstering his pistol.

Where was Earl Weathers?

Pepper doubted that the gunhand had simply ridden out onto the desert. There were no settlements in the rugged hills beyond. Logic dictated that Weathers had to return to Crater. Possibly to change horses, more probably to buy a ticket on the outbound stage and lie low until it was safe to make his escape. Perhaps he had been waiting for just such a moment as this. With Peppers out of town, the gunman might decide that the time was right to make his move.

Scowling and cursing silently at the thought of riding still more long miles across the barren land, Herb Peppers made his way down the hill toward his waiting bay mare.

Laredo's chestnut horse was walking with its head held low. The slender moon arced over and was now gradually sinking in the west. The land they travelled was barren and dusty; both horse and man were worn down to the nub by the night's ride.

Suddenly the chestnut's head went up. Its ears pricked with interest. Peering into the darkness Laredo could see nothing at first, but as the chestnut's nostrils flared with excitement, he managed to discern the low form of the Fillmore house tucked among the oak trees ahead of him. The horse moved on more eagerly now, smelling water. Laredo rode with more alertness, sensing trouble.

He was not certain of his conclusions. He sensed more than knew that the bank robbery had been a conspiracy. Amos Fillmore had done the inside work, of course, but it was Earl Weathers and his men who had gotten the money in the end. Laredo suspected that Fillmore had had more to do with things than was evident.

And he hoped to find proof at Fillmore's house.

He walked his horse silently through the dark oaks. The chestnut stepped high, energized now, eager for water. Laredo reined the animal in and sat watching the house for a long while. There was no light burning inside, at least none that he could see. It was no more than an hour before dawn. Glancing over his shoulder Laredo thought that he could see a slight grey paleness in the eastern sky. He swung down and approached the house on foot, gun in hand.

Moving through the shadows cast by the bunched oak trees, he paused every few steps and listened, but there were no sounds besides the chirping of crickets and the grumping of frogs along the creekbed.

Laredo crossed the last open space between the oak grove and pressed himself up against the wall near one of the side windows. The night had finally cooled, in this last hour before dawn, and he stood shivering slightly, holding his Colt beside his ear, barrel up. He was ready to admit that he had made a mistake, that anyone within the residence was asleep.

Then he heard the low grown coming from a room just beyond the window.

It was a pained sound, a sorrowful sound, the moaning of a person devoid of hope. Who was it though? It had to be Florence Fillmore, he thought. As near as he was to the sound, he could not tell with certainty if it had been a man or a woman's voice. There was nothing for it but to enter the house and discover what he could. He eased to the front of the house, saw no horse standing at the hitch rail, no one guarding the door.

Laredo stepped up onto the porch and crept ahead. Now he could see that the door stood open slightly, that a narrow line of faint light outlined the doorframe. The small groan sounded again and Laredo took a deep breath, toed open the door and stepped into the Fillmores' parlor.

All was dark and gloom, the furniture, the lamps only dark indistinct forms. The room was empty. He moved ahead down the carpeted hallway towards the room beyond. The dim light grew slightly brighter as he approached. He could make out the furniture there – sofa, table, lamp, and a chair where Earl Weathers sat watching him with wolfish eyes.

Laredo reflexively pointed his revolver in that direction, but the gunman's hands were both clearly visible, resting on the arms of the upholstered chair. Weathers made no attempt to move. Only his eyes seemed alert, capable.

'Are you the law?' Weathers asked in a voice that seemed to rise from a sepulchre.

'In a way.'

'You won't need that gun,' Weathers said. 'I'm finished.'

And it seemed he was. By the low lantern light the gunfighter's face was waxen, yellow. His eyes dark and brutal, sunken into his skull. He did not so much as twitch as Laredo took another step nearer.

'What did they do to you, Weathers?'

'*She*,' Weathers said, his voice only a croak now. 'It's she who did it – Florence Fillmore. Poison. She poisoned me.'

'She tricked you?' Laredo asked, not understanding. He looked around the house as he spoke, but there seemed to be no one else inside.

'Tricked . . .' Weathers coughed as he tried to speak again, a long, racking cough. His eyes grew brighter. 'You know all about it, I suppose, or you wouldn't be here. We planned it – me and Florence – kidnapping the girl and getting Fillmore to rob the bank for us.'

'Yes,' Laredo said, although that was not exactly the way he had it figured.

'She got that bumpkin, Marshal Pepper, to fall for her. Flo told him that if he kept the law out of things, she and Pepper could run off and start over. Imagine Flo with that fat clown! He fell for it, though. The damn fool.'

'So then . . .' Laredo began.

Weathers coughed again. 'Then she made a fool out of me,' Weathers said. His voice had grown weaker still. 'Here I was laughing at Pepper for being taken in by Flo's wiles. It was going to be Florence and me, you see!' Weathers said with a burst of energy. 'We made fools out of everyone: Ike and Trotter, Pepper, Flo's husband. All of them. Then she decided to make a fool out of me. We were having a drink to celebrate . . . after I showed her the money. The drink. . . .

'*Poison!*' Weathers roared, his eyes flashing with futile anger.

Then he died. Weathers' mouth was hanging open, a thread of yellow drool running from its corner. There was not a trace of the wolfish menace he had threatened others with. Laredo took a moment to ponder the transient nature of the shadows all men cast across the earth and then got back to what needed to be done.

He expected to find no trace of the missing ransom money, but he nevertheless searched through the house, focusing on Florence Fillmore's bedroom. He noticed that there was only one pillow on the bed. There were only two pairs of women's shoes under the bed, one missing a heel, the others badly scuffed. The closet was nearly empty. She had gone for good, it seemed. But where had she gone?

Laredo knew nothing of the woman's past nor of her future plans. He had no hope of finding her once she made her escape. The only thing to do was to catch her before she could get out of Crater.

She would make her try today, that was certain. Earl Weathers had been alive the evening before, sitting beside the woman, toasting their success. Therefore Florence could not have gotten far yet. Not if she was taking all of her belongings with her. It had to be the stagecoach. What time did it leave? Laredo had no idea, but he meant to be there when it loaded up.

He walked to the kitchen, keeping his eyes averted from what remained of Earl Weathers. In the breadbox Laredo found a half loaf of brown bread. He tore that apart and chewed on it as he poked abound, finding a block of cheese which he cut and ate along with the bread. He stood looking out the window at the morning sun flaring against the blue sky, casting pools of black shadow beneath the oak trees surrounding the house.

Where, he wondered, was Amos Fillmore? It was possible that Weathers and Florence had killed him, buried him in the oak grove. Laredo hoped not, not for Fillmore's sake, but for the sake of his daughter. It was going to be a sad enough homecoming for Anita as it was. Going out into the morning sunlight, Laredo squinted toward the creek and whistled up his chestnut which approached him reluctantly. The horse was worn down; Laredo could not bring himself to press on aboard the chestnut. Leading it toward the barn he passed the wheel ruts cut into the dark earth. He remembered that the Fillmores did have a buggy. Now that was gone, carrying Flo and her trunks toward the stage station in Crater.

In the corner of the barn a leggy black three-year-old horse lifted eager eyes to Laredo. Anita's horse had been missing its exercise runs and was raring to go. Laredo obliged the black, saddling the horse, walking it from the barn while the chestnut watched them blankly.

The sun was low, the road long, the black horse eager to run. Laredo heeled the pony and started at a generous trot toward Crater.

Along the way there was time for thought and speculation. He wondered if Bill and Anita had made it to Dusty's without a problem. He wondered where Pepper and his posse were. Most of his thoughts, however, remained fixed on Florence Fillmore. The deadly woman had fooled three men in her maneuvering. One of these, possibly two, were dead by her hand. She was not the sort to hesitate to kill again in order to protect her treasure – the ransom money. If Laredo could not reach the stage station before it departed, he would have to track her down no matter how long it took. The woman could not be allowed to run free in society. He patted the young black horse's neck.

'You and I may have quite a ride ahead of us,' he told it in a low voice.

Herb Pepper had been having a long ride himself. He now had blood on his hands, but still no gold in his pockets. He would kill again, he decided, if he happened to run across Earl Weathers. Kill him in front of the entire town of

Crater if necessary and justify it later. Weathers, the marshal had already decided, would be making his getaway on the stagecoach. Or, he thought dismally, maybe that was just a feeble hope. If the gunman had ridden off alone across the long desert, he was gone for good. It had to be the stage. Peppers forced himself to believe it. And Weathers could not have left earlier because Peppers himself had been in Crater, watching. It would be today.

And today would be the day Herb Pepper killed Weathers.

His bay mare staggered beneath him as they dipped down into and out of a rocky wash. Herb's fat body was slick with perspiration. He had lost his hat and the blazing sun seemed to be blistering his brain. He rode on with fierce determination, a single thought in his mind.

He still could not see Crater. He had not as yet even reached Thorne Creek. What time did the stagecoach leave? He could not remember. His overheated mind seemed to have lost some of its functions, left them strewn out across the featureless desert. Herb Pepper urged the bay on to greater speed, but the beaten horse had no more to give.

Florence would be waiting anxiously at home.

What was he to tell her if he failed? That he had failed to locate the money or Earl Weathers and that Anita was now missing? That would be the end of that. Of course Florence, being a woman, might simply pretend nothing had happened between them, go back to her ineffectual husband, see Amos Fillmore through his troubles and then either remain with the banker or play the suffering, loyal wife willingly – depending on how his trial came out.

Pepper saw no such option for himself. He had failed utterly, and it had been only days since he was projecting a brighter, wealthier future for himself. It was all the woman's fault! It wasn't, of course, but it made him feel better to ride on for a little while, cursing the wiles of Florence Fillmore. Maybe, Pepper thought, he should do the same as everyone else in the game – just find Weathers, reclaim the bank money and ride off – alone. There were plenty of other women who would be happy to share his fortune with him.

Pepper's bay mare stumbled. He tried to jerk its head up, but it was too late. The faltering horse rolled, throwing Pepper to the rough ground. He was slow in trying to rise. Flat on his back he squinted at the white skies. With a groan he rolled over and got to his feet. He slipped his Winchester from its saddle scabbard, kicked his horse and started walking toward Crater.

NINE

'But where was he going?' Dusty demanded. The red-headed girl stood with her small fists clenched, watching Bill who was sitting beside a bruised and weary Anita Fillmore lying on Dusty's sofa.

'I don't recall that he told us,' Bill said without looking up from Anita's face.

'He must have!' Dusty jabbed at her unruly hair with her fingertips and spread her arms in exasperation.

'Well, he didn't,' Bill said sharply. 'I guess he was going after Weathers. I don't know how he meant to find him, but that's the only thing that makes any sense.'

Dusty threw her hands skyward in frustration, walked to her small front window overlooking the alley that ran between the rows of cottages and stood staring toward the long desert. Where was Laredo? Riding alone after Earl Weathers and the stolen bank money. No one told her anything, Dusty decided. She still did not understand what had happened. She had not even known there had been a bank robbery – no one in town was talking about it. Where had they found Anita?

And where was Laredo?

She wanted the tall man to come back. She cared for him more than she had a right to. He had just walked into her life and briefly brightened it. Now he had just drifted away. Dusty had never thought of herself as being a lonely woman, had never felt lonely before. But Laredo's absence had triggered a deep loneliness, a yearning that she had long denied. He had to come back. Had to!

The black horse trotted eagerly on as the morning sunshine grew whiter, hotter. The three-year-old was full of high spirits, ready for adventure. Its rider rode in sullen contrast. Laredo who had gone sleepless the night before and had a stunning surprise to shock him awake in the morning was brooding, weary and angry at the world.

He had guessed right about Weathers and Fillmore – but it was the wrong Fillmore. It had been Florence and not Amos who had masterminded the bank theft. She had talked Amos Fillmore into it, preying on his love for his daughter – after Florence had seen to it that Anita was kidnapped. Then she had seduced Herb Pepper into keeping the plot quiet, to do nothing to foil the robbery. Then the woman – black widow that she was – had convinced Earl Weathers to drink a cup of poison before they fled on their fairy tale honeymoon. She was a vicious, remorseless woman; Florence Fillmore had to be stopped.

The only regret Laredo had was that she was not a man. He would have enjoyed shooting down a man who had proven so twisted and murderous. Now he thought only of catching her before she could depart. It had to be on the stagecoach; what other way was there? She had taken her trunks filled with clothing and personal objects.

He wondered distantly what would happen to Florence after she was captured. Thrown in Herb Pepper's jail, would she manage to sweet talk her way free again? Or had Pepper had enough by now? Bill Thatcher would not be around to prevent that from happening. Laredo felt vaguely responsible for Bill having taken off his badge, but it had been the young man's choice. Besides, it had been the right decision. Anita was safe now, presumably at Dusty Donegall's cottage resting and healing. Laredo thought briefly of Dusty, but he chased the thoughts away. There was no time for such matters. He wanted only to return the bank's money and to capture Florence Fillmore. And he intended to have that done before this day was ended.

The stage was running late that morning. Worse, the man at the depot said that the coach had suffered a broken axle and it would take three to four hours to replace it. Florence Fillmore flew into a rage. She berated the mild-appearing clerk, cursed the entire stage line in unladylike fashion and stormed out of the office onto the boardwalk where her baggage had been stacked. Now what! There was only one way, it seemed. She had driven her buggy and team to the Long Trail Stable, sold them to that idiot Wink Rollins and paid the simpleton and some other idler to take her trunks to the stage station. Now she was forced to try to reverse all of her carefully planned movements.

Her only worry was running into Amos who should at this time of day be firmly ensconced in his bank counting his deposit money. If Amos did appear, Florence had it in mind to simply tell him that she had had enough of him and his troubles and Crater and that she had decided to leave him.

What could that spineless man do about that? Nothing, of course.

She was also concerned with the possibility of encountering Herb Pepper. That would take a lot more manoeuvering. She had already enquired at the stable and been told that Herb was out on the desert chasing Bill Thatcher and this man called Laredo. Florence believed that Herb was really trying to find Earl Weathers – good luck finding him! The outlaw was at that moment, as she well knew, growing stiffer by the hour seated in her living room.

Florence believed that she could handle Pepper even if he should make an unexpected appearance. She had always been able to handle men. She would tell him that she was afraid to remain longer in Crater. There would be too many questions from the bank examiners, too many matters she could not explain to her husband. Yes, she loved him, but she needed to get away for a while. They could meet again later.

Of course Pepper would take that to mean only after he had recovered the missing ransom money, but that was all right. Let him think what he wanted – for the present he would be happy to have Florence out of the way where she could not be interrogated in the event of an investigation.

Supremely confident in her ability to handle the situation, Florence was only irritated as she walked back toward the stable, holding her skirts high along the dusty street, feeling a trickle of perspiration begin behind her ear on what would prove to be another devilish hot day.

Wink Rollins would be the target of her frustration. She found the simple man with the gold tooth cleaning out the stable stalls using a rake and shovel. The place stank. It was hotter in here that it was outside. Florence Fillmore was angry and in a hurry.

'I want my buggy back,' she snapped at Wink. 'And have someone go get my luggage from the stage depot. I'll also need a fresh team of horses.'

Wink straightened up, leaning on his shovel. He blinked twice in surprise as the rapid-fire orders were thrown at him.

'Ma'am?' he said, shaking his head heavily.

'You heard me,' Florence said, barely managing to keep her voice below a shout.

'Your buggy, Mrs. Fillmore? I've already found a buyer for it. He wanted the tack along with it.'

'You can't have sold it already!' Florence said, thinking that the little rat was only trying to squeeze more money out of her.

'But I have. I had a man waiting for a nice buggy for his wife and—'

'Tell him the deal is off!' Florence shouted, growing more exasperated. 'Don't you understand? The stagecoach is not running this morning.'

Wink didn't understand. The coach was seldom on schedule anyway. The banker's wife could have spent the night in the hotel and taken the noon stage tomorrow. Wink said nothing, however. He just repeated dully:

'I already sold the buggy, Mrs Fillmore.'

'Then get me another. A buckboard will do,' she said.

'I guess I've got a rig, but it's not in good shape. It . . .'

'I don't care what it's like. I told you what I want. And see that someone brings my luggage over here.'

Wink Rollins nodded. His mouth was tight. He did not like this woman, never had. If she was leaving Amos Fillmore because of his troubles, then to Wink's way of thinking, Fillmore was a lucky man. He was, however, in business to make money and he could overlook the temper of a cash customer. Wink still had the old buckboard with the splintered bed that he had purchased from Ike

Waverly when the man had decided to retire from the hauling business and go into full-time drinking. Frankly it was in bad shape, creaking, iron tires rusted, ungreased axle hubs. Unable to sell it, Wink had left the buckboard sitting out in the weather for a long time.

However, if the lady was willing to pay for it, she could have it and welcome too it.

Wink placed his tools aside and wiped his hand on a rag. The lady paced the stable floor. Wearing a dark blue dress and bonnet, her pale face was tight with determination. She was carrying one of those little reticules that the ladies toted and in her other hand a black leather valise.

'I don't know what to do about finding a team for you,' Wink said.

'Any horses will do,' Florence said sharply. 'I can handle them.'

'Yes, ma'am,' Wink responded. He believed that the lady could.

He went out to find Luke Coventry to ask him to bring back the luggage he had just unloaded at the stage depot. Luke hadn't had time to get drunk yet, and he would welcome the extra money. Wink Rollins was considering how big a profit he could make on this swap. He had to sell Mrs Fillmore a team capable of getting her out of town, little more. Wink doubted that he would ever be seeing this woman again.

Wink had nearly reached the Tooth & Claw Saloon where Coventry would be sheltering up when he was stopped in his tracks by an incredible sight.

Marshal Herb Pepper, afoot, his shirt torn open, hatless, staggering on blistered feet was making his slow way up Crater's Main Street, his eyes red and haunted. Wink had started that way to talk to the marshal when he saw Herb Pepper stop at the front entrance to the stage depot and stand eyeing the luggage stacked there. Wink saw Pepper's lips move in a slow, complicated curse, and then the marshal stamped angrily into the depot. Wink held his position and then slowly moved toward the doors to the Tooth & Claw.

Wink figured that he wouldn't be needing Luke Coventry now, but he felt the need for a drink himself.

There had long been a rumour circulating in Crater about Florence Fillmore and Marshal Pepper. In Wink's mind that rumour had just taken form and substance. At any rate, Wink did not want to be anywhere in the neighborhood when Pepper came out of the depot again and started toward the stable. He pushed through the saloon's batwing doors, figuring he had just lost some money.

Tad Becket thought at first that Amos Fillmore had not seen Pepper stagger past in front of the bank, but he was mistaken. As distracted as Fillmore had been these past few days, he was alert enough to see the fat marshal, hatless and sun-beaten, pass by.

'I'll be back, Tad,' Amos Fillmore said, fitting his hat on his head. Tad only nodded. Fillmore would not have heard any answer he made anyway. His eyes were fixed, determined. Beneath the skirt of the banker's coat, Tad saw that Fillmore was wearing a belted handgun. Tad stood at the window, watching in puzzlement. He did not know what was going on, only that it was something he needed to stay well away from.

Amos Fillmore needed to talk to Pepper, had to. What had happened out on the desert? Where was the bank's money?

Where was Anita?

He had trusted Pepper to find his daughter and return her safely. The marshal had told him that it was simply a matter of letting Earl Weathers keep the money in exchange for Anita and a promise that Amos would take the blame for the stolen money. Now here was Pepper back without the money, without Anita, without Weathers.

He damn well better have come back with a good explanation.

Hurrying, Amos Fillmore followed after Pepper. With surprise he saw the marshal enter the stage depot and minutes later re-emerge. Fillmore, reaching the depot himself, saw the leather-strapped trunk and smaller suitcases stacked on the boardwalk. He stopped dead in his tracks. The blood hummed in his brain.

Fillmore knew instantly that these were Florence's bags, of course. The question was, how did Herb Pepper know that? And what interest could he possibly have in them? The answers slowly presented themselves, confirming a deep suspicion that his conscious mind had been reluctant to give credence to.

Pepper and Florence. It made perfect sense on a logical level, but it was heartbreaking. Amos Fillmore started on again, more slowly now. There were a group of men in front of the One Tree Saloon and to Fillmore it seemed that they were all watching him, snickering behind his back.

He felt a dupe, a fool and a cuckold. He understood now, understood why Pepper had been willing to shield him. It was likely that Pepper even now had the ransom money in hand, that the two of them were planning on a rapid escape – why else would Florence's baggage be at the stage depot? Florence's bargain had not been made with Earl Weathers – not completely. The three of them had been in it together all along. Weathers for a cut of the easy money, Pepper and Florence for that, but not that alone. Had any of them ever given a thought to Anita! Angrier now than he had ever been in his life, Fillmore walked heavily on, his hand on the butt of the .38 revolver he carried on his hip.

Dusty Donegall had been about to open the door to the bank. She had been dispatched to find Amos Fillmore and give him the happy news that his daughter was safe. Anita herself could not walk that far on her torn feet and Bill Thatcher was loathe to leave her side. Dusty eagerly volunteered to walk to the bank, imagining Fillmore's joy when he was told that Bill and Laredo had saved his daughter.

Just as she was about to enter the building, however, Dusty glanced up the street and saw Fillmore making his way towards the other end of town. She turned that way, hurrying a little to try to catch up with the banker.

Looking along the street, Dusty caught a

glimpse of Marshal Pepper turning into the Long Trail Stable. Amos Fillmore strode that way purposefully. Just beyond the stable she saw a black horse she recognized as Anita's tied to a hitch rail, and saw . . . thought she saw, the tall figure of Laredo slipping into the side door of the Long Trail.

Dusty halted, gaped, lifted a hand and then rushed on, holding her skirts high. Something was about to happen at the stable, and from all indications it was going to be something very bad.

TEN

Swinging down from Anita Fillmore's horse, Laredo had stood frowning for a minute. That was Marshal Pepper who had just entered the stable. The man was hatless, his shirt unbuttoned, his eyes wild. Behind him on the street Amos Fillmore was scurrying toward the building. Was this the time to split the money – or was it a day of reckoning?

Laredo decided to try to observe them undetected. He slipped up to the side door of the stable, tried it and felt its rusty hinges give a little under his pressure. Opening it carefully, Laredo peered in. He was able to look down the aisle between the horse stalls.

Standing square in the middle of the building, illuminated by a patch of sunlight shining through the loading-dock window, stood Florence Fillmore.

There was a black leather satchel at her feet and a small silver-plated pistol in her hand. Laredo eased the rest of the way into the building, drawing his Colt from its holster.

No sooner had Laredo closed the door behind him than the bulky figure of Herb Pepper appeared in the doorway. The marshal, panting as if he had run a mile, took three steps forward and turned to face Florence accusingly.

'You dirty two-timer!' Herb Pepper bellowed, his chest heaving. 'Where do you think you're going?'

Florence had prepared for this and she answered in a calm voice: 'I had to get out of town, Herb. I can't take any more of this. The men from the bank will be back with their questions. And I can't spend another day under the same roof as that louse. With his eyes on me all the time! And what if he finds something out? He'll beat the truth out of me, won't he? He's capable of that and more. He's low and cunning, Herb. You don't know him. . . .'

Florence's voice broke off. The game was not going to play out the way she had planned it. Behind Herb Pepper now, she saw Amos Fillmore standing, listening, his eyes gleaming fiercely. There was a pistol in his hand.

'I knew it!' the banker shouted. 'Where's Anita?'

Pepper spun at the sound of Fillmore's voice. Unprepared for this, he had not drawn his weapon, now he slicked his Colt from its holster and fired one wild shot at Fillmore who returned fire. A .38 slug bored through the marshal's shoulder as the heavier boom of Pepper's .44 racketed through the stable confines. Pepper's shot was a wild one, but together the two shots created havoc. The horses, silently dozing or munching at their feed reared up, whickered and kicked at their paddocks in panic. Florence Fillmore waved her own small pistol frantically.

'You'll ruin it all, you damned fool!' she shouted. It was unclear which of the two men she was hollering at. Laredo saw her snatch up the leather satchel and turn toward him, her dark hair flying free of its pins.

'Not this way, lady,' Laredo said, and she shot him.

Laredo felt the searing jolt of the small calilbre bullet as it tore through his thigh just above the kneecap. He wobbled a little on his feet, staggering to the left. As he did Florence fired a second shot which impacted into the stable wall behind Laredo. He fired back at her off-handedly and saw Florence dive, skirts flying, for the shelter of a stall partition. The horses in the occupied stalls continued to buck and whinny, tossing frenzied heads.

Above the tumult Laredo clearly heard another shot from Herb Pepper's big bore Colt. Glancing that way he saw Amos Fillmore swat at his chest. Confusion filled the banker's eyes as he stumbled backward, his back colliding with the stable wall. He slid to a seated position, holding his hand to his chest, blood leaking between his fingers. Florence Fillmore had seen that as well. She now resumed her cajoling.

'Herb! I'm afraid. I've got the money. We can still make it out of this. All we need is two horses. . . .'

The sound of Laredo's gun firing cut off her words. Pepper had spotted Laredo standing in the shadows, and crouching, the marshal had brought his sights around in that direction. Laredo's shot missed, but it sent Herb Pepper sprawling. The fat man wriggled away on his belly, seeking shelter.

Laredo was wounded as well. Worse he was standing between two hostile guns. He moved. The rough wooden ladder leading up to the hayloft was near at hand and Laredo went that way. Climbing rapidly, his wounded leg of little use, he made his way upward. Another shot, better aimed, clipped the ladder step just beneath his foot. As he swung up and over into the loft, keeping his body low, two more shots rang out, clipping wood around him. Both of the people below were shooting at him and Laredo had no good chance of firing back unless he raised up and he was disinclined to give them a better target. He heard Florence and Pepper shouting to each other.

'We need two horses!' she yelled, her voice loud but far from panicked.

'You get them. I'll keep Laredo pinned down,' Pepper called back.

'I don't . . .' Florence began but did not finish. Laredo had the idea that she did not want to leave the money where it rested as she tried to catch up two horses. Laredo lay still, remaining patient. As things were now, Pepper had no target. Laredo did not wish to waste a shot on the concealed lawman. There was plenty of time when they were both mounted and tried to make their escape. Then he would have the clear targets he wanted.

Peering down through a crack in the flooring he saw Florence make a dash toward a wary-looking gray horse. She managed to catch its bridle, and started to lead it out of the stall. Laredo decided to put a stop to it. He fired a bullet which went nowhere near her, but was close enough, loud enough to cause the gray horse to rear again, throwing Florence aside.

'What are you doing!' Pepper shouted. He was now giving thought to the possibility that the townspeople might rush to the stable to see what was happening. Even the town marshal would have difficulty explaining the wounded man in the loft, the dead or dying banker, the mad woman trying desperately to catch up two mounts.

'I've got one!' Laredo heard Florence shout, and looking down he saw that she did indeed have the bridle of another horse, a sturdy-looking roan which was either extremely docile or deaf. 'Let's get out of here,' Florence urged. 'We can find another horse on the way!'

Pepper considered only briefly. The woman was right. The time to go was now; the method was unimportant. He peered around the corner of the stall where he had hidden himself and looked directly up at where Laredo lay.

'Lead it this way,' Pepper called. 'We'll use the horse for a shield until we hit the door.'

'Get the money!' Florence yelled back. The roan was now giving her a bit of a fight, tossing its head wildly. 'The satchel, Herb! Get it!'

The black satchel was below in the aisle not ten feet along from where Laredo had gone to his belly. Easing forward along the rough planks of the loft floor, Laredo squeezed in behind a sheltering bale of hay. No sooner had he crawled there than Pepper burst from hiding, firing three wildly aimed shots toward the position Laredo had just quit.

Gunsmoke rolled through the stable, burning Laredo's nostrils, bringing tears to his eyes. Pepper made his move, darting towards the satchel as Florence tried to hold the jittery roan. The marshal's face was glowing as he reached the satchel and stooped to pick it up.

Laredo kicked the bale of hay beside him with both feet and it slid off the edge of the loft, falling directly on Pepper's head. The marshal cursed, stumbled back and fired again into the stable ceiling. Laredo answered with a round from his own Colt. The .44 bucked in his hand and Laredo watched the impact of the slug punch Pepper backward. He fell over the split hay bale and lay still, arms out-flung.

Laredo hobbled toward the ladder and dragged himself down to the stable floor. Pepper lay still. A small, rattling sound emerged from Amos Fillmore's lips. Florence was gone. He could hear the roan's hoofs pounding along the alley beyond the building. Sucking in heavy breaths Laredo walked toward the double doors at the front of the stable, dragging his injured leg behind him. Amos Fillmore watched his progress, but that was all the life that remained in the mortally-wounded banker's body.

'Laredo!'

Laredo spun that way as the woman's voice sounded. It was Dusty Donegall, her red hair in wild disarray, her blue eyes wide with fear. She stood stock-still for a moment and then rushed to Laredo, throwing her arms around him, murmuring small wordless sounds. Dusty's eyes then fell on Amos Fillmore who still sat against the wall of the stable, life quickly leaving his body, and she remembered the task she had started out on with high expectations of the pleasure it would bring the banker.

Dusty went to her knee beside Fillmore who remained still, his useless pistol on his lap, and said to him, 'She's all right, Mr Fillmore. Anita is all right now. She's at my house.'

Fillmore was unable to speak, but his eyes brightened for a moment at her words. He reached for Dusty's hand, but death stopped his movement. Dusty looked up to Laredo with tearful disappointment. He said:

'He heard you, Dusty, he understood.'

'Then . . .' Dusty rose, smoothing out her skirt.

In the middle of the gesture her eyes widened and fixed on a point beyond Laredo's shoulder and he spun, or rather tried to spin. His wounded leg buckled under him, and as he reached for his pistol, Florence Fillmore triggered off a shot from her little pistol.

Laredo felt a stabbing pain like a red hot poker thrust through his chest below the collarbone and he staggered back, aware enough to curse himself for his carelessness. He should have known that the woman would never ride off leaving the stolen bank money behind. Laredo thought that, thought he heard a second shot echo through the stable, and then he heard no more, saw no more as he tumbled headlong into the silent black vortex that had opened beneath his feet.

The lilting voice caused Laredo to pry open his eyes. Someone was singing, and he doubted that it was an angel simply because he doubted that he would have been assigned to the pearly gates after the life he had lived, but if she was no angel, Dusty Donegall was the next best thing.

He could see her from his bed. She stood beyond the doorway, her back to him, singing in Gaelic. Laredo understood none of the words; he didn't need to or care to. Her voice was pleasant and comforting no matter the song. He closed his eyes again and drifted back into the cobwebbed world he had been inhabiting for most of the last two days.

It was already dusk when Laredo opened again opened his eyes. Dusty sat in a wooden chair facing him. Back-lighted by the deep crimson glow in the window behind her he could not see her face, but with her hands folded on her lap, her patient watching was soothing.

'I been giving you much trouble?' Laredo asked and Dusty jumped a bit, startled by his voice.

'No. Not much. Though you do talk in your sleep some.'

'Do I?'

'Yes, but don't ask me to repeat what you were saying.'

'I won't.' Laredo tried to hitch himself up into a sitting position but found his shoulder and leg both uncooperative.

'You'll be hurting for quite some time,' Dusty said. She rose to her feet, came to the bed and propped an extra pillow under his shoulders. She turned then to light the bedside lantern.

'Jake Royle will be mad,' Laredo said. 'He thinks I get myself shot up occasionally just so that I can take some time off the job.'

'It's not much of a job if it takes that for you to be able to relax a little now and then,' Dusty commented. She returned to her chair, refolded her hands and leaned forward slightly, watching Laredo.

'It's a good enough job,' Laredo said around a yawn. 'What happened back in the stable, Dusty? Mrs. Fillmore had me.'

'Amos Fillmore's pistol was still on his lap. When Florence lined up for a second shot I took the gun and shot her dead.'

'That's twice you've pulled me out,' Laredo said. 'You're kind of handy to have around.'

'You bet I am,' she said with pride. Then, 'I'm sorry that I killed Florence Fillmore, Laredo. I know what she did, but still I wish it hadn't been me.'

'You probably saved a lot of other people some grief,' Laredo considered. 'Is everything all right at the bank now? I mean, they did get all of their money back, didn't they?' he asked.

'Most of it, Tad Becket says. Some of the money was missing. They figure that Earl Weathers spent some of it for supplies: food, whiskey and such.'

'Sure,' Laredo answered. 'Did Anita go back home yet?'

'Bill wouldn't let her go at first. And it was a

good thing he didn't,' Dusty said with animation. 'Do you know what he found when he went out there?'

'Yes,' Laredo said, 'I do.'

'Anita was staying over at the Crater House while she healed. Mostly because her feet were cut up, you know? When she started feeling better the first thing she wanted to do was go riding. She was pleased to find that the black pony was already in town – oh, by the way, Bill found your chestnut horse out at the Fillmore place and he brought it back to town and put it up at the Long Trail. So I guess you'll owe Wink Rollins some money when you're up and about again. I took your horse for a ride with Anita, I hope you don't mind. I had Mrs Tompkins – you don't know her – sit with you while I was gone. Wink said he'll trust you for the money, realizes now that you weren't after his gold tooth. But he wasn't so sure that Florence Fillmore wouldn't have taken it given the chance, the way she was . . . I'm talking a lot, am I not?'

'You are.'

'I've always done that when . . . I think it's when I get nervous, Laredo. I think that's what does it.'

He nodded, fixed his eyes on hers and said thoughtfully, 'Maybe if we both put our minds to it we can find a way to keep you from getting so nervous.'

That seemed to make Dusty even more nervous. She went on, though not so rapid-fire as previously.

'I don't think you should keep on in your line of work, Laredo, do you? I mean you are tempting fate. We should just write that Jake Royle a letter and tell him you've had enough.' Dusty became more eager, telling him, 'I really do have a lot of money, Laredo. People used to think that I did, but then they saw the way I lived – the way I wanted to live – and they decided that it was untrue. But I have it. I could buy a house, buy land for a fine ranch.'

'And I could sit on the porch all day in my rocker?' Laredo asked with an ironic smile.

'I don't think anyone could keep you down,' Dusty said quickly. 'But I just . . . wanted you to know, Laredo.'

The woman was cornering him, or trying to and Laredo knew it. Luckily at that moment there was a knock on the door and Bill Thatcher swaggered in, looking none the worse for wear. There was a marshal's badge pinned to his leather vest.

'Re-enlisted, I see,' Laredo said and Bill reddened a little.

'Yes, well, there's no one else around to take

care of business with Pepper gone. I told the town council that I'd take the job for a little while. See how it fits now that I don't have Herb Pepper over me.'

'You'll do fine,' Laredo said, meaning it. 'How's Anita?'

'Now that she's over the shock of everything, she seems fine. She's scrubbed that house from top to bottom.' Bill frowned. 'I'm afraid it all may be just busy-work, though. I don't think she'll ever be comfortable in that house again, Laredo. I've sort of had my eye on a little cottage not far from Dusty's. . . .' He reddened again and Laredo said:

'Congratulations.'

'It will be good for the two women, having each other nearby, don't you think?'

'It will – if she's going to stay here,' Laredo said, turning his eyes toward Dusty who shifted uncertainly in her chair.

'Why wouldn't she?' Bill asked in puzzlement. 'Where are you going, Dusty?'

It was Laredo who answered. 'I don't think we've quite decided that, Bill. When we make up our minds, you'll be the first to know.'